A HEART'S DESIRE

KRIS MICHAELS

KMRW LLC

A Heart's Desire
By
Kris Michaels

Agent McKenzie is nobody's 'yes' boy and has the letters of reprimand to prove it. He smells the stink of political maneuvering in this case and he can see the handwriting on the wall. Hell, the words are three feet high and written in crayon. Someone in his own agency wants a target on Liam Mercier's back but McKenzie would be damned if he'd put one there.

The damaged man currently in his custody needs his protection, not manipulation. That's why he'd agreed to use a safe house that was off the grid. Throwing away his rarely used FBI procedure book had nothing to do with the protective urges he felt around Liam. Nope, not a damn thing to do with heavy doses of desire, or spikes of lust. He was just doing his job, after all, he has a killer to catch and a victim to keep alive. Protecting his best bet of taking that sick bastard down was his civic duty.

Forced to face the nightmares of his past or lose his pension, Liam Mercier did the only thing he could do. He walked back into his personal hell. The man assigned to protect him is everything Liam wanted and needed—four years ago. Leaving the small island of sanity he'd been existing on could cost him everything. But being hunted by a genius, sadistic killer without the protection of the sexy, intense, agent was a guaranteed death sentence. Fate had dictated Liam's course four years ago. The only thing he questioned was when his killer going to finish his work.

CHAPTER 1

*A*gent Steele McKenzie stood outside the interview room door and took a deep calming breath. The initial sensory overload of this crime scene required a deliberate pause. Splattered arcs of blood contrasted obscenely with the stark white walls. A spray of crimson-brown blood had coagulated and dried in shallow pools on the cheap table. He'd been doing the job long enough to be jaded. But this one? The gore alone would probably garner national attention and undoubtedly a heavy dose of pressure from his superiors at the Bureau. This case was so much more than a bloodbath.

A demand from one of the crush of hospital administration types kept behind the crime scene tape drew his attention. The self-important officials didn't stand a chance at getting past the uniformed patrolmen, although a few thought they were important enough to try. Didn't they know they'd made themselves persons of interest by virtue of their presence? Probably not. Fucking trolls.

His attention returned to his victim. Mutilated and eviscerated, what was left of the dead body was loaded into a body bag—hopefully, one that was leak-proof. The coroner continued his work in the confined interview space. Steele watched him place the last scooped-up pieces of the remains into the body bag before he closed it. Stench from the victim's sliced bowels assaulted Steele's nose. After five years as the lead investigator for the FBI's Serial Killer Task Force, he knew what to do. He pulled air through his mouth, almost negating the wretched smell of the blood, bile, and dissected bowels. Almost.

The forensic element of Steele's team worked in concert with the coroner, collecting and photographing evidence, sorting and lifting prints. His investigators scattered throughout the facility. Two took statements. A third ran the hospital personnel's schedules to ground. Steele slipped a pair of clean crime scene booties over his shoes and entered the room, careful to avoid any contact with trace or blood evidence. His focus centered on the victim, and in particular, the time the killer had taken to gut him.

Steele mentally cataloged every detail as he moved in a methodic, concentric search of the small room. The barbaric son of a bitch. Just when you think you've seen it all you get... fuck, you get a monster like Stuart Miller.

"Chief, got an update," Masterson called to him from the door.

"Give me a minute." Steele did the heel and toe dance to navigate the gore and exit the crime scene without disturbing any evidence.

Masterson was one of his investigators, and the man had a gift. People told Sam things they wouldn't tell another soul. Personally, Steele believed his slow southern accent and good looks somehow charmed interviewees, both male and female. The soft drawl made people think he wasn't an intelligent, laser-focused investigator. The ability to get people to open up, coupled with the fact that Masterson had great investigative instincts and a rock-solid work ethic, won him a spot on Steele's team.

"All right. Go ahead." Steele deposited his used booties and latex gloves into a crime scene hazmat bag.

"We've finished with the orderlies' statement, nothing helpful. We'll confirm they were doing what they said they were, but it appears they're just typical drones doing the job. I did find out the subject was on a course of antidepressants plus a regimen of antipsychotics. The staff noticed no difference in him today. Brought him down for his mandatory psychiatric appointment. Bastard's routine hadn't altered in over a year. The nurses and orderlies said over the two-and-a-half to three years he's been here, the man mellowed. He became so sedate on his meds that the administration decided he no longer needed restraints. I've got the list of the drugs the man was taking and will submit them to the lab. Chief, he has a *seven* hour lead on us. They did an internal search of the facility when they found the doc dead. Of course, that was before they called us in. That sick son of a bitch is dust in the wind."

Steele's attention locked onto Masterson. "Sam, find someone in personnel who can locate Caleb James. He was the lead agent for the team that captured Miller and he has background on this case. Arrange an immediate meeting and any travel necessary. I want all court transcripts from Miller's trial. Get me case notes, psychiatrist reports, and a copy of all evidence—not only the evidence submitted to the court but also the shit that they held back. I want all debriefs on the first task force team members and physical locations for them now."

Masterson hesitated for a split second before he headed down the hall, scribbling his field notes as he walked. The FBI wouldn't have jurisdiction in this case had it not involved Stuart Miller—a sadistic serial killer known as the

Heart's Desire Killer, HDK for short. Disgusting how the national media was now reducing abominations of nature into catchy monikers.

Steele's mind ticked through the info he remembered from the original case. He'd studied it prior to agreeing to take the job as lead agent for the current task force. Steele's predecessor and his team had captured Miller. The lead agent had retired as soon as the HDK case closed. The team that worked it had scattered into other positions within the Bureau or had retired.

From what he could recall, Stuart Miller was a white male and would be in his mid-to-late forties. The sick son of a bitch's trial had been publicized and blitzed across every major network. The cameras portrayed the man as polite, quiet, and utterly forgettable. Shades of Jeffrey Dahmer, David Berkowitz, Dennis Nilsen or Gary Ridgway. Not a person you'd recall for any apparent reason. Miller came from an upper middle class family, had worked as a nurse anesthetist prior to what psychiatrists had assumed was a major psychotic break. According to timeline recreations, one day Miller had just left his job and assumed a new persona. With a dead person's ID and social security number, he'd melted into society and become a transitory drifter who'd traveled the south. He'd moved from job to job, working as a mechanic in businesses ranging from high-end hot rod garages to chop shops.

Miller's killing spree had led the task force on a manhunt that spanned years. Two agents had been killed and one critically injured during the serial killer's takedown. Counting those two agents, Miller had been charged in the deaths of fifteen men. The fun fact of the day? Nobody knew if Miller had more victims. The fuck-wad was found guilty and didn't say a word in his own defense, during his interviews or at his sentencing. That he was criminally insane was a guarantee.

The fact that he was a sadistic lunatic and a criminal genius who got off on torturing and killing gay men and was now free was what scared the shit out of Steele. You just can't predict how *crazy* will act, and that made his team's job almost impossible. Almost.

The starting point would be what the team had done to capture Miller five years ago. The original team had caught Miller in the ritualistic act of carving up his fourteenth victim—an agent and a member of Caleb's own team. That agent lived. There was a shit ton of history he needed on the case, but what Steele wanted to learn most was what had transpired to decimate the previous task force. Losing a member of a close-knit team usually brought people together... unless the team already had issues.

The leadership at the Bureau had shut him down when he'd asked about the team he was hired to replace at the beginning of his tenure. The good ole boys slapped his ass with a letter of admonishment when he'd ignored their original decree to stop looking. When he'd continued after the admonishment, they'd threatened a reprimand and removal from his newly-appointed position. Steele had filed the knowledge that the brass was hiding something because he liked his new position and the information made no impact on his current work. So, begrudgingly, he'd stopped poking the bear. But something had torn that original team apart, something the Bureau didn't want known. The higher-ups were covering up a black mark of some sort. He'd bet his last dollar on it.

A not-so-discreet cough had Steele's gaze drifting up to his agent who hovered by the door. He raised a questioning eyebrow at his newest agent. Her sharp angled haircut, harsh black business suit and lack of make-up couldn't detract from her waif-like presence.

"Chief, the doctor who was hacked up in there today was

filling in for the regular psychiatrist. The usual guy, Doc Sands, was married yesterday and is either just now landing in Hawaii or in the process of screwing his new wife in his honeymoon suite, depending on whether it is a six- or seven-hour difference."

"Six hours due to daylight savings, and good work on the tact. You're improving."

She snorted. "Hey, I could have said fucking her brains out, right? Yous guys know me. I keep it classy." *Waif-like? Not so much.*

Steele shook his head at Agent Fleming's Jersey-accented directness as she continued, "Anyways, the victim was a fill-in for Sands. Semi-retired, fifty-seven-year-old consultant, name of... Dr. Peter Anderson. No family, wife died three years ago. That was the only schedule change in this ward. Sands requested this leave of absence six months ago. According to the security system, Miller used Anderson's ID card to exit the facility. And natch, since it's Memorial Day, there was only bare bones staff working. Nobody saw anything out of sorts until an orderly noticed Miller was still out at shift change."

Steele nodded his head and turned back toward the room. Same story as Masterson was getting. Nobody saw anything amiss. He watched one of his forensics team step over a piece of... yeah... intestine. Steele glanced back to his agent. "I need to know who in this facility processed that vacation request. Was it common knowledge the doc was leaving? Did the staff talk about it in front of patients? What computer database held the vacation information? What type of security is on the hospital information systems? Are days off posted on boards? Where are duty schedules built, maintained, or displayed? Everyone who had any involvement will be interviewed—no exceptions. Call Doc Sands and ask him if he told Miller he'd be out. And for God's sake, get me a copy of all the video this place has for the entire day. No stone unturned, Angela." Fleming scribbled furiously as she headed down the hall.

Masterson nearly collided with her as he approached with his phone plastered to his ear. His brisk conversation terminated as he reached Steele. "Chief, we have Caleb James' home address—an hour's drive from here. Also, somebody high up is looking for you. The office gave me this number—said you were to call it immediately."

Steele took the slip of paper and pocketed it with his phone, which was off—for a reason. He'd make the call to whatever brass object was trying to interrupt his investigation on the drive to James' house.

They left the facility twenty-five minutes later, Masterson was driving while Steele pulled every string he had to get the electronic files of the original case sent to him immediately. His phone nearly exploded when he turned it back on. Seven missed calls from the same number Masterson had given him.

He pushed redial and closed his eyes. Not because he was tired. No, he closed his eyes because he didn't want to see his imminent death coming. Masterson was a damn good partner, but the man could not drive for shit. He'd survived maniacal killers, but Masterson's driving? Well, it was a pray-and-wait situation.

"About fucking time you called." The angry voice clipped in his ear.

"Seriously? Who the fuck is this?" Steele sat up and glanced over at Masterson.

"This is Caruthers." Steele slammed his head back against the headrest. Fuck him dry, what in the hell could the division chief want from him?

"What's the status on the Miller case?"

"Well, *Sir*, since I've only been on the case a couple of

hours the status is we are investigating." Masterson snorted and coughed out a laugh. Steele sent him his best 'you are going to die' stare, but the smile on Sam's face just grew bigger.

"Let me save you some time. The man who is the key to catching that son of a bitch is an ex-agent. He's on a medical pension. As far as we're concerned, he's still on the payroll. Get to him, and use him to get that fucker back in custody."

Steele's gut reaction was to tell the guy to fuck off and let him run his own investigation, but Caruthers held a shit ton of power, so he'd play. For now. "Use him? Sir, he doesn't even have to see or talk to me. How the hell do you suggest I *use* him?" Steele grabbed at the dash, propping himself back against the seat when Masterson hit the brakes suddenly.

"If he doesn't cooperate with you, I'll question the legitimacy of his pension payments, and we'll strip them from him. Make no mistake about it; Liam Mercier is the bait you need to set a trap for that monster Miller. This case has attention at the highest levels and I have my superiors' full backing. Use Mercier. Get Miller." The line went quiet. Steele looked at the phone.

"The fucker hung up on me."

"Who was it?"

"Caruthers."

"What did he want?"

Steele pocketed the phone. "Me to pull a fucking rabbit out of my hat. Other than that, I haven't got a fucking clue, but he's willing to put a former agent out on the line to get this bastard. Something stinks, Sam."

"What are you going to do?"

"My job."

"Smart." Sam laughed and jammed on the brakes again.

Steele grabbed at the dashboard again and prayed he'd make it to Caleb James' house in one piece.

~

HIS PREDECESSOR WAS *NOT* what he expected. Steele accepted a cup of coffee and tracked Caleb James until he sat down—lanky, with close-cropped blond hair streaked with gray. A nervous tick pulled at one of his brown eyes.

"The Bureau didn't say *why* you were coming over, McKenzie. What was so damn important you pulled me off the golf course?"

Steele leaned back in the chair to watch the impact of his words. "Stuart Miller escaped just over eight hours ago."

Caleb's face went slack and lost all color. A ghostly shade of gray appeared where a pink flush had once resided. The older man swayed in his seat before he put his head in his hands. "Where's Liam? You're arranging protection, right? Have you notified him yet? Is he okay?"

Deep-seated emotion rode the urgency of his questions. Steele blinked at the man across the table. "He'll have protection, but to answer your question… we haven't contacted him yet." Steele had pulled up an electronic copy of the medical report on Mercier and he damn well knew the reasons his team chief was concerned, but he wanted to hear it from the agent's mouth.

Caleb's hand shook before he clenched it into a fist and stuffed it in his pocket. He turned and peered out the window. The man cleared his throat twice before he spoke. "McKenzie, if Stuart Miller is out, the only way you are going to catch him is through Liam. Liam's a"—his eyes darted toward Steele—"well, for lack of a better word, I'd guess 'savant' will suffice, especially when it comes to that fucker. We tracked Miller for years and we got nowhere. I brought Liam on the team and let him run with his hunches. His methods worked. We were closing in."

"What happened? How in the hell did Miller abduct a

member of your team? How did he abduct Liam Mercier? The back office won't disclose it."

The older man closed his eyes and shook his head slowly. "I didn't control the situation. Liam figured out Miller's base of operations—his torture facility. I didn't... I should never have..." Caleb's shoulders dropped and so did his voice. "I didn't know how to deal with what was happening on my team. Some pretty serious shit was going down. Mercier was smack in the middle of the situation. It divided my team, and to be honest, I had no idea how to talk to Mercier about it. I mean, I knew he was the same guy, but that's not... Anyway, I thought he was trying to plead his case, so I deleted his voicemail."

A single tear trickled down the man's cheek. James didn't attempt to wipe it away. "He told the doctors during the debrief that he'd called me and asked for backup. Fuck, McKenzie, that demented son of a bitch held Liam captive for thirteen days. Miller's only words after we finally had him in cuffs were that he was going to get to Liam and finish it. Those were his last words to us."

His voice trailed off as his eye tick raced wildly. "He held his victims for fourteen days, what he did to them, to Liam... then he... Damn it, McKenzie. I signed a non-disclosure statement. I can't say anything. I'm fucking bound by a gag order." Caleb's voice rose in anger. "Have you read the fucking case file? Seen the pictures? Do you know what he did to *my* agent? To *Liam*? Because *I* fucked up?"

Steele nodded, watching Caleb's mannerisms and reactions. They told him more than words ever could. The remorse for not having done his job was evident. So was the man's gut-wrenching certainty *he* was the reason one of his team members had been tortured.

"McKenzie, that bastard carved into him, left scars. He's one sick mother. Why haven't you told Liam?"

Steele took a drink of the coffee that Caleb had provided. "Even if Miller knew where Mercier was now and had the means to drive directly there, he'd never make it before we get to Liam. We've got the airports and bus stations covered. Don't worry, Caleb. There is a plane waiting for me, but first I want your notes—the real ones, not the sanitized version in the case file."

The older agent pushed back from the table and started pacing along the counter. He cast glances at Steele. Apparently Caleb was trying to determine how far he could trust the agent seated at his kitchen table. McKenzie didn't have time to coddle the old man. "I need the notes, James. Time won't stop, nor will Miller. If I'm expected to keep Liam alive, I need everything and I need it *now*."

Caleb nodded and walked to the back of the house. He returned with a box filled with documents and a thumb drive. He slid both across the table.

"I'm violating my agreement by giving this to you, but McKenzie, this information... Nothing I can do now will fix what my ignorance did then. Liam won't talk to me. He won't... not that I can blame him. If anything in here helps you, then maybe a slight redemption of my sins is possible. You're team lead now. Make sure you take care of him. I didn't. No, that's not right. I wouldn't... and I have lived to regret my actions."

Steele stood gathering the materials, but Caleb stopped him, handing him a business card. "This is Liam's doctor. She's been treating him since the incident. The Bureau is footing the bill, so she'll talk to you. Besides, Liam signed the waivers when he first started therapy. Talk to her before you speak with him. It will help you understand where he is... mentally."

Steele pocketed the card without looking and turned to

leave. Before he pushed open the screen door, he paused and glanced back over his shoulder.

"I agree Miller is obsessed with Mercier, but don't let your guard down, Caleb. Everyone who had a part in putting that lunatic away is a potential victim. My team is contacting the rest of the original task force. If you see anything suspicious, don't hesitate to call it in."

"McKenzie?"

"Yeah?"

"If you can find a time or a situation, let him know that I'd change places with him if I could. I don't know how to make it right..." The older man turned to look out the window.

McKenzie felt for him. "Some things just can't be fixed, Caleb."

"I know." The comment carried through the screen door behind McKenzie.

CHAPTER 2

"*I*t's a risk I don't think you should take, and yes, I know you're just following orders. But you don't understand the extent to which this man has been violated." The shrink was adamant and the conversation once again circled to her obvious disagreement with what he had to accomplish.

McKenzie turned his head and stared out the window of the private jet. The crystal blue sky and bright sun did nothing to elevate his dark, foreboding mood. In a perfect world, this conversation wouldn't be happening, but his hand had been dealt, and unfortunately he needed to win with only one card—Liam Mercier, his ace in the hole, so to speak. Steele cringed. No, that wasn't true. The man was the whole fucking game.

His ear buds helped to keep the conversation between Dr. Morgan and himself private. He didn't want Mercier's business laid out for public consumption, even if 'public' in this instance was his teammate of three years. So, while McKenzie dealt with the shrink, Masterson pretended to sleep. He acted oblivious, but Masterson was sharp; he'd have a good idea of what was said from Steele's side of the conversation. A small snore stopped that assumption. Steele drifted a glance toward Masterson. The man was gone. Drool pool gone.

Steele chuckled to himself and focused on the questions he needed answered. "I've read the initial reports. What's the bottom line here? What do I need to know? How do I approach?" Steele asked.

"Honest and direct. He's not a suicide risk—now. It was touch and go for a while. You'll need to give him time to process what you're telling him. Don't bum rush him or pull any macho he-man routine. He's isolated himself for a reason. Besides that, he's more than a little paranoid. He's damaged, but he's worked damn hard to get a grip on his life. If you do what the Bureau wants, because you're there with him *you'll* be on the hook to keep him safe. Put my number on speed dial and don't fuck this up, Agent McKenzie. Liam's life is on the line. Miller isn't your only worry if you start down this path."

"*When* I start. I don't have any options." Steele drew a deep breath and closed his eyes. His recent viewing of Liam Mercier's crime scene pictures flashed through his mind. The fact that Mercier could still function stood as a solid testament to the man's internal strength. Steele knew he'd have to move slowly and cautiously, but hearing it from the doctor was a kick in the balls. He'd been sent to do a job and that job required him to open old wounds. Sometimes he hated the world he lived in.

The doctor's sigh broke through his musings. "Look. At one time, this man was on the fast track. His performance evaluations were always firewalled. He maxed out in every category."

"I saw that in the background I pulled. Listen, when we were talking this morning, Caleb mentioned a situation that pulled his team apart. What can you tell me about that?"

"Officially? Nothing. But if you are asking for my assumption I'll give it to you."

"Tell me what you know, doc."

"All right. Well, in my opinion, it wasn't the situation that caused the problem that divided his team. Caleb's response is what tore the team apart."

"Care to elaborate?"

"Liam Mercier is gay. He was outed by a fellow task force member. The way it was done was malicious and if I had to guess, intended to destroy any chance Liam had at advancement. Agent James' lack of response sealed the team's polarization on the issue. Even if Miller hadn't been captured, that task force was done."

"It isn't against regulations to be gay." Steele's jaw hardened as his jaw tightened, grinding his teeth.

"Nope, but it is against policy to have relations with a superior. The allegation was Mercier was sleeping with one of the big boys—a highly visible, married, big boy. I don't officially know who it was, but he was so high up that a gag order came down on the team, hard and fast. James refused to talk to Mercier, so the poor man couldn't dispute or acknowledge the allegations. The facts would have come out in an inquiry, but by that time the big boy's reputation would have been tainted. From what I understand, the big man involved took an immediate leave of absence and worked a deal that allowed him to retire quietly. If you want to know who the player was, that's your bread crumb trail. It's not hard to marry the date of retirement with the incident. That's how I found out. Liam never said whom he was involved with, but he was left to defend himself, even though the superior was the one who should have been prosecuted for sleeping with a subordinate. So—"

Steele finished the doctor's thought. "So when Mercier called James to let him know he'd made a break in the case, James thought the call was about the situation and deleted the only way of finding Mercier."

"Until they went back through Mercier's notes at his apartment. It took them forever to decipher Liam's short-hand. But the thing you need to focus on is that when he didn't show up for work the next day, nobody checked on him. Caleb James violated just about every supervisory ethos in the book. He's lucky he was allowed to retire. In my honest opinion, the man should have been charged with criminal misconduct. Liam Mercier was abandoned by the people who should have had his back."

"This just gets better and better. Thanks, Doc." He hoped his sarcasm didn't drown the good doctor.

"Oh, hey, anytime." Apparently the dripping sarcasm didn't faze the doctor. Her soft chuckle in his ear seemed relieved. "Listen, just take care of him. Nobody has ever done that, McKenzie. He'll expect you to disappoint him simply because everyone, except Phillip, has done just that. Prove him wrong. If he knows you have his back, maybe he'll be able to do what you need him to do."

"Phillip?"

"Yeah, they're inseparable. If you want Liam to go with you, you'll need to make sure you take Phil."

"Great. Just fu... Just awesome." Steele ended the call but didn't pull the ear buds. According to the doctor, Liam Mercier was damaged but not completely broken. The man needed to be handled like a cracked piece of china. On his best behavior, Steele had as much tact as a raging bull. Maybe... On a good day. Hell, his team had a well-deserved reputation for a complete lack of said tact. On his office credenza, the letters of reprimand sat right next to his team's commendations for outstanding work. At the Bureau, everyone knew one 'oh-shit' canceled out a couple of 'atta-boys'. Steele had a sense of pride that he'd been able to keep his team ahead in the tally with a couple of pats on the back still in the bank.

Mercier in his care? Not a good combination. But, he'd fucking deal and he'd give Mercier what he needed to get him on board. Because Miller would kill again and keep killing until they stopped him. The fact that Miller's ultimate goal was Liam Mercier gave his team leverage.

≈

THE COMPUTER CHIRPED, drawing Liam's attention back to his work. Another paper submitted just under the cut-off. He glanced at the monitors, checking his security systems before he moved the new work on his thesis to the external hard drive. A wisp of hair escaped the leather tie he used to pull the length back. Damn stuff. He hadn't cut it in almost five years, probably never would. Liam shuddered at the thought and forced his mind from that path. With two clicks of the touchpad he posted his daily assignment on the class boards. The pursuit of an online doctoral degree filled his days. Gave him a purpose. He found he enjoyed pushing the boundaries his electronic professors set, pressing buttons because he could. The small rebellions fueled his recovery. He could feel his successes. He'd actually moved forward —finally.

Dr. Morgan had laughed last year when he'd told her of his hobby of harassing the professors, pointing out their mistakes and challenging their reliance on rote dogma rather than experience in the field. She'd applauded his efforts but wanted him to step outside his comfort zone. She'd challenged him to do something utterly radical. So he did. He adopted Phillip.

As if triggered by some invisible signal, a reverberating rumble shook the air before His Royal Majesty jumped into Liam's lap and bumped his regal head under Liam's chin.

"I just have to think about you and you show up. You, sir, are definitely a pain in my ass." Liam reached around the long-haired cat after he'd given an initial swipe down the animal's silky fur. The Maine Coon's chirpy trill came back at him, almost as if the cat was speaking to him. As usual, His Highness had decided Liam was done working. His verdict given, Phillip launched onto the workstation and used the corner of one of his laptop screens to scratch his cheek.

"Happy with yourself, aren't you?"

The cat flicked his tail to and fro, trilling and chirping his response. The massive feline carefully navigated the expansive workstation. Liam glanced at the clock and once again checked his security systems before he headed into the kitchen.

"Okay, come on. Dinner for you, workout for me." He heard the soft thud of the cat's weight landing on the floor behind him. The last time the mobile vet had been here the brat weighed close to twenty pounds. Should he try to put Phil on the treadmill? Liam laughed at the bizarre thought. *Maybe I've finally lost my mind.*

Phil wound around his legs impatiently chirping until Liam put his food bowl down. Mandatory chore of the day done, Liam headed into the second bedroom. He'd set up a gym for himself—a rowing machine, a Phil-less treadmill, and free weights. Turning on the monitor over the rowing machine, he scanned the six security camera feeds before he changed to work out.

Halfway through Liam's run, Phil jumped onto the room's only windowsill.

"Better watch it. I'll have you logging miles if you're not careful."

Putting on his best act of disdain, Phil ignored him. Within minutes, he'd stretched majestically across the entire length of the windowsill. The cat thumped his tail, soaking in the warmth of the spring sunshine. Phil loved the late afternoon light filtering through the decorative wrought iron bars. His neighbors had decried the addition of the window bars, complaining that the neighborhood was safe and the implication it wasn't brought down their homes' value. Like he'd given a shit. He'd encase the house in cement and never leave if he thought it would keep Miller away, but nothing would. It was a certainty. Miller would come for him and he would finish it. The only question was when.

Liam cursed, pushing the thoughts away. He'd crawled through dark times trying to live again. According to Dr. Morgan, he'd been in a holding pattern. Healing. Progressing. Liam transitioned to the row machine, then free weights. Today was a leg day. He hated leg day. Deadlifts, lunges, and squats sucked. Phil stretched in solidarity. At least Liam assumed it was solidarity. Better be, or the fur ball was getting dry kibble tomorrow.

∼

"This is it?" Steele studied the house that sat at the end of a small spur off the main road.

"Yeah, according to the records." Masterson pointed to the address listed in the GPS on the dash and lifted Mercier's case file to double-check his home address. "Not what I expected."

Steele did a quick sweep of the area before he spoke. "Yeah, me either. But then again, after what that man has lived through? Hell, I'd live in a fucking bunker too."

Steele threw the car into park and eyed the structure. Iron bars covered the windows and formed a protective barrier at the front door. There was no yard. Crushed rock surrounded the small building, creating a three-hundred-foot clear zone. The peeling paint of the squat house lay in stunning contrast to the other well-maintained dwellings lining the road. If he lived next to this hovel he'd be pissed. Mercier's property definitely took the price point of the neighborhood down a notch. The man probably didn't give a shit, and honestly, Steele couldn't blame him.

Masterson opened his door as Steele did the same. "Hey, Sam? Hang here. This isn't going to be an easy conversation."

"I don't know, chief. That's not standard operating procedure." Masterson hesitated, halfway out the door.

"Look, this guy isn't the enemy. He's a former agent who put his life on the line to capture a fucking serial killer. I don't need backup, and maybe this guy could use a break. Just stand down."

"Don't like it."

"Don't care."

"Didn't ask."

"Know it."

"Fine."

"Fine."

Steele chuckled as he crossed the expanse of crushed rock. Masterson's personality had probably dropped his lover's defenses more than once, but thankfully, they weren't each other's type. The men Sam gravitated to were big guys —huge mothers who could consume a man. And fortunately, neither Sam nor he were drawn to the frail type. No way would Steele want a man he'd end up bruising if he held him too close. He liked strong men and preferred them attractive too. The front door opened as he stepped onto the porch,

catching him in mid-thought. He liked a man... Well, hello...
That was what Steele liked.

Liam Mercier held a .45 automatic against his thigh. The
matte finish of the weapon against the light gray sweats was
a warning—one Steele would heed. Mercier had his finger on
the trigger and Steele could plainly see that the safety had
been flipped off. The man's expressive eyes locked onto
Steele's with a cautious, almost fearful, gaze. His tall, hard-
planed body wasn't disguised by the long sleeved T-shirt or
sweatpants he wore. No, the man was built, and everyone
could see it, clothes be damned.

Mercier stood at the home's threshold framed by the
peeling white paint of the door casing. The drabness of the
house accentuated the beauty of the man—long blond hair,
big dark brown eyes, straight nose and full sexy lips. Fuck,
the man's face and body hit every hot button and checked
just about every box for Steele. Liam Mercier could pose as
an archangel and nobody would dispute his right.

"Leave. Now. I'm following the agreement. I haven't done,
or said, anything—to anyone." The man's smoky-soft timbre
carried the distance. *Holy hell.*

Steele cleared his throat. "Ahh... Okay. I'm not sure why
you think I'm here, but I can guarantee you nobody thinks
you've done anything wrong."

"Credentials." Liam lifted the automatic a fraction. The
intent... noted and understood.

"Reaching for them, two fingers... Not trying anything,
man." He slid his hand slowly into his inner jacket pocket and
retrieved his creds. "There you go. Supervisory Special Agent
Steele McKenzie."

Liam grabbed the leather holder and flipped the ID. Civil-
ians would never think to look at the back, but that's what
he'd do. A forger wouldn't worry about the reverse of the
card, face value only. A quick glance at the hologram on the

back of the creds and they were airborne, heading back at him. Steele caught the leather holder easily but didn't pocket them.

"What do you want?"

"Can we talk? Inside?"

Liam shot a glance around Steele. "Leaving him outside? Not SOP."

"Yeah, I didn't figure you needed anyone else around for this discussion."

Steele watched it happen. The man in front of him folded in on himself—not physically, but mentally. Liam's eyes lost the spark he'd seen for the past couple of minutes. The natural blush that had graced the man's cheeks seconds before withdrew, leaving a sickly pallor.

"Miller?"

"Yeah."

"Shut the door." Liam turned and walked into the house. Steele heard the handgun's safety click into place as he pulled the door closed behind him and trailed Liam down a hallway. The alarm panel beside the door chirped when the door secured, echoing past the silent trek both men completed.

Immaculate. The word sprang to his mind when he took in the interior of the small home. The furniture was old, well used, but everything was clean. The front room boasted a wall of flat screens that currently monitored every angle of approach to the house. His rental vehicle and Masterson were on display on the largest screen.

Liam stopped with his back to Steele. The screen on the upper left showed the living room. Steele couldn't scratch an itch without Mercier knowing it.

"Please… Tell me he's dead." The whispered plea turned like a knife in Steele's gut.

"He escaped early this morning."

The man swayed, but steadied himself against the wooden desk.

"Thank you for coming to tell me in person. Please shut the door on your way out. I'll lock it from here." The mere breadth of volume came out as more of a prayer than a request.

"We need you to come with us."

Mercier shook his head, sending his thick blond hair in motion. "No. I won't leave here. I can't. I can keep him out if I stay here."

"Without a doubt. You've got a fortress, but the Bureau needs your help on this case. You're the only one who could figure out what this bastard's next moves were. We need to catch him before he kills again."

"No." Liam ground out the answer.

Shit. "Look, the Bureau will contest your disability retirement if you don't agree to help." A first-class prick of a move, but one he'd been instructed to use. When his superiors had told him what they would do if the man balked, he'd wanted to puke. Fucking bureaucracy. Mercier lived on a fixed income and apparently the majority of his money went toward his security. Taking away his income would force Mercier to get a job and make him even more vulnerable.

In basic terms, Mercier was fucked if he didn't help and bait if he agreed. He just didn't know it yet. Or maybe he did. The man used to be an exceptional agent.

Liam shook his head and pulled the tie out of his hair. His fall of blond hair swept across his shoulders. His hand swept back the hair that dropped into his face, flexing his bicep under the dark blue, long sleeved T-shirt. Standing closer, he could see the man actually wore two T-shirts. Why he was dressed in layers was beyond Steele. The interior of the house was uncomfortably warm.

Mercier sat down and planted his head in his visibly shaking hands. "He'll finish it."

A statement of fact. Steele couldn't deny Liam would be walking straight into the path of a madman who wanted to kill him. That declaration headlined every counseling transcript of Miller's he'd reviewed.

Steele had only one ace up his sleeve, so he used it. "I'm not Caleb. I'll protect you."

"He told you?"

"He gave me his original field notes. I know you were set up to take a fall by a superior. How long had you been with him?"

"How long? How about once? I didn't know who he was. He didn't say and I didn't ask."

Damn, so the superior was being watched and Liam fell into a shit hole. "I'm sorry for what happened before, but you don't need to worry about me doing the same thing as Caleb."

"Just words. I don't believe you. I won't... I mean, I can't. You just don't understand. One day I'm his number one agent. The next? Thirteen days. Three hundred and twelve hours, eighteen thousand seven hundred twenty seconds. Every last one spent in hell because he... Words. Words... just fucking words..."

"Listen, we'll take Phillip with us. I'll foot the bill if the Bureau won't pay. We need you to work with us. Help us catch Miller. You won't be alone this time." Steele winced internally as he used Liam's partner to sweeten the deal, but Liam acted like he hadn't heard a word.

Steele bent down, taking a knee in front of Liam. The man's face was still buried in his hands, thick blond hair draped, blocking any view of his anguish. Steele brushed a finger across Liam's knee, causing the man to jerk and push away with a surprised gasp.

Steele lifted his hands in a gesture of surrender. "I'm sorry, I didn't mean to startle you. Listen, the reason I understand what it did to you when Caleb turned his back on you is because I'm gay. I'm out and I don't give a flying fuck who knows it. My team isn't like your old team. None of us will let you down, but *I* am the team lead for this task force. I. Won't. Abandon. You."

"You know what Miller did to me?" Liam's pupils had blown wide, the chocolate brown of his eyes almost entirely swallowed by the black of his pupils.

"I do. I've read the reports."

"I'm afraid." The utter hopelessness in the man's admission damn near broke Steele's heart.

"I know."

"I can't."

"You'll stay with me. Twenty-four seven. We'll protect Phillip. He'll be there for you when you need him. I won't leave either of you alone for a moment." He could make that promise. Until they caught the son of a bitch, he'd let Liam attach himself like a leech if it would get the killer off the streets.

"He'll kill you to get to me."

"I'm hard to kill."

"I'm not afraid of dying. It's what he'll do before I die."

"Yeah. I get that. Come with me, Liam. It's time to stop letting that bastard control your life."

Liam stared at him. The searching depth of those brown eyes fused with his. Hell, Steele had no idea what the man was looking for, but evidently he'd found it, because he pushed out of the chair and headed toward the back of the house.

Steele trailed him and admired the view. Liam was worth watching—a high, tight ass that would fit perfectly in his hands. He sighed and rolled his shoulders. The man didn't need him lusting after him. The delicate bubble around Mercier's world had been shattered not more than five minutes ago. Steele gave himself a mental punch in the face, a good hard one. Get through the case, then maybe, when the bastard was behind bars again, he could consider the option of pursuing Liam. Steele leaned against the doorjamb as Liam threw a small suitcase on his bed. Fuck, the heating duct blew hot air directly on him. *Damn it, it was hotter than hell in this house.* Why in the hell did Mercier keep the thermostat set at sun-scorching sweat-bath?

"Dude, is your heater broken?"

Liam paused, a long sleeved T-shirt grasped in his outstretched hand, suspended over the small travel suitcase. For several seconds, it hovered, giving away a pronounced tremble. "No. You said you read the reports."

"I did."

"The cold. I…"

Son of a bitch. If he could physically kick himself in the ass, he would. Miller. The sick fuck.

"All right. I'll make sure we keep you warm. For the trip back, will jackets work?"

"Yeah."

What other triggers would Liam have? The case file detailing the torture… He needed to review it again and try to sidestep any potential landmines. He'd call Dr. Morgan as soon as he had a moment alone. Maybe she'd be able to give him a heads-up on how to interact with Liam's triggers. Right now, he'd walk softly and be honest like he'd been advised. It seemed to work. Steele moved away from the vent.

The bedroom was squared away, nothing out of place, bed made and no dust. Liam packed shirts that had been pressed into exacting squares, socks and underwear folded and placed just so in the case. His ironed jeans hung in measured intervals in the small closet. They were folded neatly and laid over the rest—precise, immaculate, and controlled.

Liam retrieved items from the bathroom and closed his suitcase. He stood in the middle of the room looking at the floor for a few moments before he headed back to the living room. It was as if the person had disappeared and the shell that once housed the man went through the motions of closing up the house and setting the alarms.

"Where does Phillip live? We'll stop to get him. You should probably call and give him a heads-up."

Liam stopped messing with his computer system for a moment. He glanced over his shoulder and Steele could swear he almost smiled. "Who told you about Phil?"

"Dr. Morgan."

"You've been doing your homework, Agent McKenzie. Just not enough. Phil is a cat. A therapy step Dr. Morgan insisted I take." He looked toward the hall and lifted his chin. Steele glanced behind him and jumped.

"Shit, man! It's freaking huge."

Phil sat with his tail curled around his feet and chirped at Steele.

"Dude, it doesn't even meow. Are you sure the thing is actually a cat?"

"Pretty sure."

"How the hell are we going to take him?"

"Cat carrier."

"You got one?"

"Yeah. Brought him home in it."

"Can you get him back in it without a tranq gun?"

"We'll see."

"Shit."

"Yeah."

Twenty minutes and several painful but non-life-threatening scratches later, Steele and Liam exited the small house. The man he'd been tasked to retrieve had shut down. Liam didn't talk, he didn't ask questions and he didn't look at either Masterson or himself, not during the ride to the airport or the flight back. Well, the Bureau was getting what they wanted. Liam Mercier had been coerced into leaving his sanctuary. How much use would the man be? Who the fuck knew?

CHAPTER 3

*A*ngela Fleming stood waiting at the end of the psychiatric hospital's vacant corridor. They'd kept this wing of the facility closed, much to the administration's disapproval and angst. According to Caleb's notes, ensuring that Liam saw the murder scene exactly how it was when it was discovered was essential. The man's methodology in processing a crime scene bordered on bizarre, but it had been extremely effective. Hopefully, it would be again. Tension and fear rolled off Liam in waves, the force of the emotions tangible, so much so that Steele could feel the man's anxiety like a palpable, physical presence. Steele's gut rolled with the feeling he was leading Mercier to the electric chair or the hangman's noose rather than a crime scene.

"Agent Fleming, this is Agent Mercier."

"I'm not an agent." The first words the man had spoken since they left his house. Well, at least Steele's quasi-abduction hadn't completely shattered him. In the five hours since they walked out of Liam's house, he'd wondered, more than once, if it had. Seriously, how much more could Liam take?

Hopefully a lot more, or Steele would be front and center when the man imploded. Wouldn't that be fun.

He needed to focus on what the doctor told him to do. Okay, he'd given reassurances that he wouldn't leave. Steele racked his mind for a 'non-threatening' way to let the man know he wasn't alone. Fuck, he was completely out of his element.

"Liam Mercier?" The look of shock on Fleming's face was quickly concealed but completely obvious to both Steele and Liam.

"Yes." A subtle raise of an eyebrow, no emotion—void, absent.

"Great to meet you. I'm Angela."

∾

LIAM ACKNOWLEDGED *and* dismissed the woman with a brief nod. To say he didn't want to be here was the understatement of the millennium. He'd popped an anti-anxiety pill before they'd taken off and had downed another one when they landed. God, the second one had better kick in soon or he was going to lose his shit. He'd used every therapy technique he could recall to keep it together on the plane ride. The pills would get him through the crime scene. They had to. He turned to the interview room where he'd been briefed that the doctor had been murdered. The yellow tape sealed the room, leaving the crime scene still intact.

A wave of unadulterated terror splashed across his exposed, brutalized nerve endings. Chills contracted his muscles, clenching viciously at his gut. The reality that Miller had stood in this hall, not twenty-four hours ago, doused a fresh wave of terror over him. Oh God, he wasn't going to be able to deal… He needed to get out. Now.

Liam cast quick glances down the fluorescent-lit hallways. An inner voice screamed at him to validate Miller wasn't near. No, no he needed to run... but to where? God, he needed air. He had to get away from here. Miller would know. He would know the Bureau would pull him in. Damn it! He'd count on it. It was a stupid move, bringing him here.

Miller would finish it.

No, that couldn't be right. The Bureau wouldn't do that to him.

Liam jumped as Steele's hand settled on the small of his back. The agent was checking his email on his phone, not paying attention to him, yet the simple, possessive, reassuring contact grounded Liam's escalating fear. He wasn't alone. Agent McKenzie had sworn he wouldn't abandon him. But he'd heard that before.

The small, terrified voice in his brain screamed at him not to trust anyone. To get out. Yet the overwhelming desire to flee abated with the warmth of the agent's reassuring hand.

A flurry of activity to his left drew him out of his swirling thoughts. Fleming handed Steele a set of gloves and booties. She turned and extended the same to him. His heart slammed in his chest as he slowly backed away. *No... God, no...* In a slow motion fog, Liam watched as Steele pocketed his phone and pulled a latex glove over his hand.

Liam doubled over. He was going to vomit. Oh God, the smell of the latex. Bile surged from his stomach to his throat. Acid burned his throat and the back of his mouth. *Miller used latex gloves when he... Oh fuck.* Liam lunged down the hall to a trash can by the water fountain.

His gut lurched. Projectile retching wrung every ounce of strength from his body. Steele's strong hands held his hair from his face and rubbed his back when the rolling wave of nausea hit again. Torrents of expelled bile reduced him to a trembling mess over the hallway trash bin.

"I'm so fucking sorry, Liam. I would do anything not to bring you back into this hell. But we need your help. We need you to go into the room." Agent McKenzie's soft words breached the misery that squeezed the breath from him.

Liam slumped to his knees and tilted to his left, propping himself against the wall. He swiped his mouth with his sleeve. Tears and sweat trickled down his face. How could he be sweating when he was so damn cold? He wrapped his arms around himself. *The cold. Oh God, please... not the cold.*

Steele reached to move a flop of hair from his face with his gloved hand. Liam rounded in on himself and retched beside the waste bin, but there was nothing left to heave.

"Gloves... Get away." Could Steele understand his moaned plea?

"Okay, no gloves." Steele rubbed Liam's back and the thought of the smell on his hoodie spurred him into a frenzy of action. He pulled the thing off and threw it.

"Fuck!" He crumpled against the wall.

Steele backed away and pulled off the glove, tossing it in the vomit-splattered garbage can. "Fleming, come over here. I need to go wash my hands. Stay here with him."

"You got it, chief." The woman's sensible black shoes appeared in his line of vision before she sat down beside him. She didn't speak, didn't touch him. Thank God. He needed time. But that was the one thing Miller wouldn't give him. They didn't understand. How could they? How would he tell Agent McKenzie the truth? His truth? Liam dropped his head to his knees, trying to pull himself together.

"Here, have some gum." He lifted his head and took the silver-wrapped offering. The cinnamon flavor beat the burn of the bile in his mouth.

"Thank you." His voice sounded deeper than usual, probably from the force of his projectile vomiting.

"Forget about it. We've all have bad days."

Liam clamped his jaw shut. The urge to scream at the woman's idiocy assailed him. *Who in the hell was she to assume her bad day could ever measure up to any of the days in the last five years of his fucking life?* He dropped his head to his knees, once again blocking out the world with his hair. Endless days stretching one after the other. Months without human contact. Fear of opening the door for the people who delivered his food, his Internet purchases or his—God forbid—neighbors. He never initiated conversation, except with his doctors, and that was via computer chat. Bureau docs had long ago agreed to his long distance counseling. He didn't do face-to-face, yet he'd opened the door this morning for the FBI agents parked in his driveway. Deep down he'd known why they were there. It had only been a matter of time.

"Liam, we should try now." Steele's voice brought him back to the hallway where he sat. The woman was no longer beside him. How long had he been sitting here? Liam lifted his head, acknowledging the agent's words. Steele held out a hand, but Liam couldn't bring himself to touch a hand that had been covered in a latex glove. He shook his head and lifted off the floor. Intellectually, he knew the damage Miller had inflicted on him caused his reactions. Intellect didn't cause him to puke up his guts. Fear did. Liam drew a deep breath. Hard to believe he was actually conscious. Small victories, as Dr. Morgan would say.

Liam closed his eyes, breathed deeply and nodded. Steele cut the tape and Fleming opened the door using a bootie instead of a latex glove. He would've thanked her, but the sight of blood spray on the walls pulled him forward.

This wasn't right. The obscenity of the kill wasn't normal for Miller. What he saw in this small room was a statement of rage—one of dominance. Miller was a finesse killer. He took pride in his work—the precision of the cuts, the pain he could inflict, and the terror he could wield. This kill was

different. Primal and grotesque, not the artistry Miller
aspired to in his kills.

Liam spoke over his shoulder. "Close the door, please."

The door snicked shut and Liam shivered. *So damn cold.*
He pulled the sleeves of his T-shirt down and tried to bury
his hands in the material. The splashes of dried blood and
voids where the organs had been collected were confusing.
This wasn't Miller's usual MO, so he was sending a message.
But what? Where and to whom? This scene had to have a
purpose. Miller always had a purpose. Twisted and sick, but
always an underlying reason. Liam's body shook uncontrol-
lably. From the cold or the stress of the moment, who knew?
He sure as shit didn't.

Liam stepped over a dried brown bloodstain and backed
into the right-hand corner of the room.

"I've seen Miller do the exact same thing on just about
every one of his interview tapes." Steele's voice broke the
silence, too loud and sudden in the confines of the
small room.

Liam nodded, acknowledging the comment but not the
hidden question. He didn't want to talk about what he had to
do to get into Miller's head. The agent needed to be quiet. If
he had to do this shit, he wanted to get it done and get the
hell out of here. Home. Back to his alarm system, iron bars,
deadbolt locks with reinforced kick plates, motion activated
camera system, and an arsenal of guns. Back to his illusion of
safety. But for now, he needed to concentrate.

~

STEELE WATCHED as Liam lifted a hand to his mouth and
tapped his lips with his index finger. The exact mannerism
Miller would use when being asked questions by the doctors
before they stopped taping the sessions. Liam's eyes blinked

repeatedly and the muscles in his face went lax. His breathing went short and shallow and became the only sound in the room. Steele focused on Liam. Although he stood in the room, Liam wasn't present—or maybe just not in the same reality Steele stood in.

Moments ticked by that turned into minutes. The buzz of the overhead lighting, annoying and mechanical, grew louder and wrapped around Mercier's shallow breaths. A real fucking concert. Had Steele pushed Liam too far, too fast? Caleb's notes said Liam would work through each angle in his head before he'd brief the team. Was he working through the crime scene or had he retreated to a safe place in his mind? The man stood like a statue, muscles frozen, with the exception of the blinking of his eyes as they scanned the room—a huddled shell in the corner of the room.

Without warning, Liam straightened and walked from the corner to the interview table. He sat in the same chair Miller would have sat on. Steele knew that bit of information, but there was no way Liam would. Mercier looked at the crime scene and evidence photos Steele had placed on the table, studying each intently but not touching anything.

"Where was the pen?" His voice was soft, almost a whisper. The anguish Steele heard slammed across the room.

The urge to protect this man from any more pain washed over McKenzie. He could sense that Liam sat on a razor's edge. He didn't want to be the reason the man lost the fragile grip he had on his life—the one he'd fought to carve out. Steele knew it and so did Liam.

"I don't think there was a pen recovered." Steele pulled out his phone and double-checked the evidence inventory. "No, no pen."

Liam lifted his hand and pinched the bridge of his nose. "This doctor didn't work from a computer, tablet, or notebook. Look at the photograph of the papers on the desk. *Where* is the pen, Steele?"

The agent in him understood the question but not the concern. "A pen wasn't recovered. Maybe Miller took it."

"No, no, no, no... Think, *damn it*, think. This is his *message*." Liam covered his face with both hands and started to rock back and forth in the chair.

Steele reached out to comfort the man, but the instinctive reaction froze with Liam's sudden lurching movement. Liam shoved back the chair and dropped to his hands and knees. He scanned the room on all fours. Leaning to look under the table, he flinched as if he'd been shocked by an electrical current.

Liam stood, pushing back into the corner. He wrapped his arms around his waist and slid down the wall. He lifted his arm, index finger pointing toward the table. "The pen."

Steele dropped to his knees. A piece of paper had been folded and stuck into a joint under the table, hung like an ornament. One word was visible. *Liam.* The pen had been driven deep into the wood's seam on the underside of the table, holding the note up out of view.

~

FORENSIC TECHNICIANS PHOTOGRAPHED the evidence and carefully removed the paper, unfolding it after they'd placed it in an evidence bag in order to save any trace material that might fall from the paper. Steele glanced at the paper. The words were simple and clear.

MY BEAUTIFUL LIAM, you are still my heart's desire and it is time.

Fuck. The sick bastard. Steele ducked out of the room and cast a quick glance for Liam. The man had backed himself into the corner of the hall and pulled his long sleeved shirt tight against his muscled frame. Steele pulled off his suit jacket. As he approached, Fleming backed away from where she'd posted herself.

"May I?" He lifted his jacket in an offering.

Liam stood unmoving except for the shivers that ravaged him, no acknowledgement that the man had even heard him. Steele wrapped the coat around his broad shoulders and allowed his hands to linger on Liam's arms. Liam's eyes widened in surprise and he moved away from the contact. Understandable. He'd nearly been killed by the reactions of homophobic assholes—fellow agents, the ones who were supposed to have his back. The same people who for most agents became as close as family, closer sometimes. They'd take a bullet for you because you'd step in front of one for them. Liam's teammates had violated that unspoken code. No wonder he'd pulled away.

None of that mattered now. Liam needed warmth. Fuck the world if they had a problem with Steele providing it. He pulled Liam into his chest and wrapped his arms around the shivering mass of tense muscles. After nearly a minute, Liam leaned into his embrace and that small release just about gutted him. A low, almost inaudible, groan vibrated against his neck. The man who had once been a rising star in the Bureau trembled in his arms. Steele pulled him close and ran his hands up and down the shifting plates of muscle of Liam's back, trying to provide comfort and warmth at the same time. Liam attempted to pull away, but Steele moved a hand to the base of the shaking man's neck, holding him close.

"I've got you. You don't have to worry. You're safe."

"You can't know that. Nobody can. He'll finish it. He

won't stop until he finishes it." The rumbled words muffled against Steele's chest. The hopeless comments triggered every gene of protective DNA in Steele's body.

"He'll stop if he's dead. If I kill him, he can't hurt you."

∼

LIAM TUCKED his head into the crook of Steele's neck and shuddered. The pure horror of the crime scene had been irrevocably etched in his mind. Standing in the corner of the room, he'd seen the blood spray pointing toward the table. The flow of the splattered streams would draw one's attention to that point of the room—to the table. Something had been off. He'd seen the evidence in the photos. Sitting in the chair, he had seen the letter 'p' to his left swiped with a fluid scroll of crimson blood. Miller had wanted him to find something that started with the letter 'p'. Evaluating the photos, he'd racked his brain for an answer. The lack of a pen had been the only thing he had been able to find. It had been like that when he'd tracked Miller before. The sick fuck had baited him, teased him and taunted him. Today, a hard fought piece of his existence had melted away when he'd stood in that corner and forced his mind to play Miller's sick games again.

The heat radiating off Steele McKenzie wrapped around him and cloaked his body in blessed warmth. If they weren't standing in a hall he'd have burrowed into the man. He was so damn cold. It wasn't frigid in the hall. Intellectually, he knew that. But the gripping ache from a cold he wouldn't forget never left him. Steele had wrapped his massive arms around his shoulders and pressed their bodies together. The confinement became a heavenly cocoon of warmth.

The agent meant well, but he couldn't stop Miller. "He won't kill me until he finishes it." Liam tipped his head. His lips caressed the base of Steele's neck as he spoke. An accident, but the contact seared the air between them. So damn good. It had been years since he'd been held. He'd been alone for so long.

~

FINISHES IT? That was the third or fourth time Liam had said those words. He needed to get Liam out of here, give him some distance. Somewhere he could feel safe—if the man actually ever felt safe. Steele dipped his head and momentarily pressed his cheek into long blond hair and whispered, "I *will* protect you."

Steele understood that Liam had suffered. At least he understood in theory what had happened, based on the reports he'd read, although the statements Liam had given while in the hospital were threadbare at best. Since the Bureau had DNA evidence *and* had caught the sick mother in the act, they hadn't needed to rake one of their own over the coals to get a conviction, one of the few times Steele could remember the Bureau doing the right thing when it came to the people involved in cases. Although, knowing what he knew now, it had probably been because they hadn't wanted the reason the agent had been captured to come to light. The FBI's motto of Fidelity, Bravery, Integrity only went so far, especially since the Bureau knew shattered lives could be reconstructed. As long as convictions were chalked up, sacrifices were expected.

Justice at all costs. Steele got that. He did. But sometimes the price of bringing people to justice could be too damn much. Liam had already paid, and now the Bureau, *his* Bureau, was asking the man to pay again.

Steele had his homework set out before him tonight. You'd think thirteen years in law enforcement would have desensitized him to the horrors of humanity, but Stuart Miller had taken torture to a previously unknown level of perverted. He needed to piece together what the sick bastard had done to Mercier based on the photos and detectives' reports of the other victims. Maybe it would give his team the edge.

Mercier stopped his violent shaking but Steele didn't let go. The man he held needed him. God, Liam fit perfectly against him. *And that shit needs to stop.* Catching Miller needed to be his primary focus. If he could catch Miller, he'd keep Liam from dangling as bait. He needed intel and insight. In order to get that, he needed to get Liam to talk to him, to trust him. True, his plan used Liam, but not in the way the Bureau's plan would. That counted for something, didn't it? It had to count because Steele didn't know if he could be the one responsible for putting Liam on the hook. Yet he knew he'd be forced to do it if his plan didn't produce quick results.

$\sim$

LIAM TURNED his face and gazed down the long corridor. A tall Hispanic man strode down the hall to where he stood wrapped in Steele's arms. The man's self-assured walk had a swagger that told the world he knew he was on top of everything. Great. All he needed was someone else to witness the tragedy that was Liam Mercier.

He tried to pull away again, but Steele tightened his grip slightly. He could break free if he wanted. The warm hand at the base of his neck didn't tighten enough to threaten him, but it let him know it was all right to stay. Permission. God, the thought stunned and comforted him.

Liam turned his head, hiding behind the fall of his hair. Five years ago, he would have been the strong one, the one offering comfort and giving orders. Now he couldn't even tolerate the smell of latex gloves. Once, he would have been working the case, not the shaking leaf clinging to the lead agent like the man was his only lifeline. Liam had stopped being that confident man five years ago. Maybe it *was* time for Miller to finish it. He was so tired of being terrified. Was he exhausted enough to give up? Maybe. Besides Phil, did he have any reason to keep fighting the agony of waking up or the terror of sleeping?

Steele's calloused thumb started a methodic sweep along the side of his neck. Liam focused on the rhythmic motion. The sensation pulled him from the dark thoughts that swirled through his mind.

The stranger's footsteps halted and the man's throat cleared. "Chief, we've been monitoring missing persons reports in the tri-state area. We've had two that could be associated with Miller reported as missing in the last twelve hours. One is a forty-five-year-old father of three. The local LEOs suspect the man may have left a volatile situation willingly. The other is a twenty-seven-year-old teacher. We think the teacher is a possible victim. He fits Miller's MO."

"Get that info out. Fleming is in the other room. Get with her and get up to speed on the new lead."

No, no, no. That was wrong. They were chasing the wrong things. Wasting resources. It would only give Miller more time. Speaking up was a risk. But Steele had said he wanted his help. He'd asked.

Liam drew a breath and spoke quietly. "Ahh... no... I think you're wrong. Don't chase those leads. This... it's too soon. Those men probably aren't his. He'll acquire one, but not right away."

Steele's body tightened under his hands. *Damn it.* He should've just kept his mouth shut. Maybe he could go home? He didn't want to be here. He really needed to leave.

"What would you do if you were in charge of this investigation?"

"Why?" Liam pushed his mop of hair away from his face as he stepped back.

"Because you know this man better than anyone on the planet. I want to know what you'd do next. I need your help on this."

Oh. Steele didn't give off the mannerisms of someone trying to humor him. Maybe the agent actually wanted him to consult. So far the man *had* been truthful, at least as far as Liam knew. He'd determine that later. Reserving judgment on anything happening right now fell in the realm of a solid plan.

"Don't use your resources on those missing persons." His throat was still sore from his glove episode and his voice sounded like he'd gargled with rocks.

"Come on. Let's go sit down. I'd like to talk through that response with you."

Steele led Liam into a small conference room away from the crime scene. The fluorescent lighting danced off the wood veneer of the cheap table. The cold, hard plastic of the chairs would have been intolerable if not for Steele's suit jacket. Liam pulled the coat tighter against the chill of the room. Because it was cold… wasn't it?

"Okay, Agent Mercier, if you were in charge of this investigation, what would you do?"

Liam glanced up at Steele, then over to the three agents standing behind him. Masterson pulled out his notebook. The woman, Fleming, and the newcomer leaned against the wall. Those two didn't want him here. Join the club. He'd leave if Steele would let him. Maybe. He couldn't know for sure if his house remained secure. He hadn't received an alarm on his cell, but that didn't mean anything. Miller's intelligence went beyond genius… whatever that was.

He cleared his throat and moistened his lips. "Let the locals chase the leads on the two missing men. If Miller returns to his original MO, he'll need time, money, and supplies. He'll most likely steal the surgical and medical equipment he uses. I'd work with local burglary units along the most direct routes from this facility. It's a starting point, but that's not his only game. I found security footage of him based on a reported sighting from the tip hotline."

"How many calls did you get on the hotline, and should we set it up again?" Masterson's voice interrupted Liam's thoughts.

Steele lifted an eyebrow questioningly, so Liam answered. "Hundreds. I was desperate, so I tracked what felt like the most reliable calls. Yeah, I'd get the word out on his escape to the national networks. He's a ratings bonanza. They'll plaster his face across the nation and we'll get calls."

Liam concentrated on the table, his mind ticking off operational strategies. He continued in a distracted voice. "He may loiter in the emergency room of a large hospital waiting for a trauma to come in or an incident to take place in the ER. When it hits, he'll use the chaos to get in the staff-only areas. Once in, he knows what he wants and walks out with what he needs."

Liam looked up at Steele. "Stick to populated areas with urban sprawl. If you don't get any leads, work the smaller municipalities. If he starts collecting again, his equipment is essential and it will be the second thing he goes after."

Liam straightened in his chair. *This* he knew. This he could do. With renewed confidence he continued. "But first he needs a place. If he's out, he already has an idea of where he's heading. Remember the man is a genius. He played us for years and was right under our noses. If he sticks to his MO, he'll look for warehouses or factories that have refrigeration units. It doesn't matter the condition. He'll get them working again. Old or broken doesn't matter to him. Isolated isn't a requirement. The victims aren't in any condition to cry out for help. If you have a theft of surgical supplies, target the area. Do a survey with the local electric company to see if there are any unexplained power draws at abandoned facilities or houses. That's how I located him. If he makes another addition to his collection—if it's not me—whoever he takes will look like me, or like I did five years ago. He has a type."

Liam's eyes lifted once again to Steele's. The understanding and respect he saw firmly etched on the agent's face stripped away some of the mental exhaustion weighing on him. No longer casually leaning against the wall, the agents pored over their phones and notebooks. The scurry of activity centered on Steele. The lead agent's voice rang through the room, sending his minions racing. Liam pulled the borrowed jacket around him, tightening his grip on the lapels, and glanced at the clock on the wall.

A vivid thought punctuated his consciousness. No matter his intent, the agent currently commanding this team couldn't stop the course of events Miller's escape had initiated. Miller *would* come for him. Miller had whispered his sick words of admiration and love with every slice of the scalpel. If they didn't stop Miller, he'd finish his work and Liam would die.

Not that he'd been living, in the ordinary sense of the word. He'd existed on painkillers, then antidepressants, for a couple of years. After his initial statement, he'd never been questioned by any law enforcement entity. Liam couldn't say what information he'd given during that interview. Minus a patchwork swirl of fractured memories, he didn't recall the first six weeks after he'd been rescued. The disjointed images following that didn't make much sense.

His doctors said it was a protection mechanism. Too bad he couldn't forget the thirteen days Miller had held him.

That metal table, the unbelievable cold... the excruciating pain... unable to move, to get away. Listening to that sick fuck hour after hour as Miller carved through his skin. A shiver of revulsion and a waterfall of saliva hit him. God, he couldn't throw up again. Concentrate on something else.

Phil.

That poor cat bastard was probably royally pissed.

Phil needed to be let out of his carrier.

The uniformed officer left to cat-sit didn't look like he appreciated the job.

Did hotels accept animals?

Where would Phil end up if Miller won?

No, wrong thoughts.

Dr. Morgan challenged him to get the royal pain in his ass cat.

Maybe he'd write out a will and leave Phil to her.

God, that would serve them both right.

Morbid, probably shouldn't go there, but so damn funny.

Almost worth dying to see.

"Hey, you ready to go?"

Liam jolted at the words and swung his gaze away from the craptastic fake wood-grain tabletop he'd been locked on. "Where?"

"Somewhere safe."

"My home?"

"No. Need you to stick close to us. Besides, I don't think Phil needs any more airplane stress today." Steele motioned toward the door as he spoke.

"Since when did you start worrying about my cat?"

"I've got to admit, that saber-toothed tiger is impressive."

"Going to sell him to a zoo?"

"Nah, I decided I'd try to make nice. I'm going to charm him. I think he may be worth some effort." Steele's smile seemed sincere.

"Yeah? When did you decide that?"

"About the same time you decided you'd start working with me. Look, the place we're staying isn't tied to this team. Even if Miller connects you to me, he couldn't make a jump to where we're going. If Phil doesn't like it after he sees it, we'll try something else. Deal?"

"I don't know. Phil's a discerning type of cat. Some would call him difficult." Liam was enjoying the banter and relaxed a bit as they walked.

"I think he'll be okay. Besides, he's exhausted. Been an eventful day."

"Yeah." *Wasn't that the understatement of the week?*

"No doubt. Come on." Steele motioned toward the exterior doors.

"Want your jacket back?"

"You warm?"

"No. Hardly ever."

"Then keep it." They walked out the hospital's main door, their voices echoing in the emptiness of the night.

"Can I get it tailored? Sleeves are too long."

"Smart ass."

"Astute. Who made you an investigator?"

CHAPTER 4

*K*ing Phil was, in fact, royally pissed. He growled and hissed at Steele, striking at him with his needle-sharp claws when Steele tried to 'charm' His Majesty. The cat's movements shook the plastic carrier and motivated the brave FBI agent to sit in the front seat, which was fine with Liam. The traffic kept Masterson busy, and apparently Agent McKenzie's phone required his attention. Liam closed his eyes, leaning back against the cloth-covered seat. He wouldn't sleep tonight without a pill, but at least he could pretend now and distance himself from the men up front.

Distancing himself from Agent McKenzie... not likely. Seeing him on his front step this morning—in that suit. From head to toe, every nuance of the man radiated an innate and smoldering sexuality, which McKenzie somehow wrapped in a perfect manifestation of utter confidence. Each inch of his muscle-bound six-foot-six inch body molded that suit fabric into a delicious cornucopia of expensively tailored treats. The body under the suit held his attention. Steele's dark hair, blue eyes, and dimpled chin were the delicious frosting on one hell of a man-cake. Sex in a suit. The man mounted a full-on assault on Liam's depleted and anemic social skills. *Mounted. Ha... funny.* Five years of therapy and all it took was one sexy-as-sin agent for his dick to decide it finally wanted to play. God, how ironic. Just when Liam started coming back to life, Miller forced him to look straight into the face of death. Again.

The enormity of today's events had more than once threatened to overwhelm his ability to cope. McKenzie's thoughtful kindness and reassurance helped keep him in one piece—albeit, one puking, shivering, withdrawn, broken and ragged piece. God, how humiliating.

The heat of his embarrassment crept up his neck. Once he'd been driven and filled with the same justified zeal Liam saw in Steele's team. Now his immediate goal centered on not needing another pill to stave off a panic attack and praying one sleeping pill would knock him out for the entire night, both of which were entirely unlikely.

Within ten minutes, Phil's purr shook the carrier more than his previous temper tantrum. Steele cast surreptitious looks at the animal and his eyes swept over Liam with each glance. He knew that because he watched the agent through his eyelashes. Another wave of shame washed over him as Steele's eyes traveled over him. It was too dark in the car to read the expression his eyes held. God, Liam hoped it wasn't pity.

The car slowed dramatically. Liam lifted off the seat and blinked as he did a double take. Masterson pulled up to a twenty-foot-high wrought iron gate. As he worked the keypad, Liam peered down the driveway. Nothing but mani-cured green lawn stretched as far as his eye could see. Masterson drove without any hesitation or indecision. He'd obviously been here before. As they pulled over a large hill, Liam caught a full-on visual of the four-story colonial mansion. White columns, black shutters, the manor reminded him of the *Gone with the Wind* estate but on a T-Rex-sized batch of steroids. The expansive sweep of green lawn and sculpted bushes played background to a massive water fountain centered in front of the huge building.

"Who lives here?" Liam gaped at the massive gated compound.

"Lucifer Cross gave us permission to stay at his east coast estate." Steele said the name as if every FBI agent in the country had access to the house of one of the world's greatest rock musicians. House? Hell, the place would qualify for its own zip code. Masterson followed the perimeter road toward the back of the compound leading to several small houses centered snuggly behind the behemoth four-story structure. The average-size homes settled contentedly in between an Olympic sized swimming pool, tennis courts and what appeared to be the first tee of a golf course. The vehicle pulled into a drive and stopped.

Liam exited the car and did a three-sixty. The splendor that surrounded him left him breathless.

"Makes you feel small, doesn't it?" Steele's voice startled him out of his dazed viewing.

"Absolutely insignificant. How did you get permission to use this place?"

"Sam. He and Lucifer have a relationship." Liam cast a look back at Masterson, who'd taken off toward one of the houses with his bag and Phil.

"Relationship? As in Lucifer, the lead singer of the Sixth Element, is gay?"

"Relationship, as in I-have-no-idea-and-I-didn't-ask. He's touring Europe and Sam just made a call to get permission to use one of the houses."

Liam pulled Steele's jacket closer and shuddered. "You're cold. Come inside."

"No."

"No? You want to stay outside?" Steele's eyebrows shot up in surprise.

"I mean, no… I'm not too cold. Sorry. I'm… Hell, I don't know, maybe out of practice?"

Steele allowed only one eyebrow to arch. Oh, that movement was sexy as fuck. "Out of practice?"

"With talking and being around people." Liam drew a deep breath and looked down. The weight of the day crushed around him, sapping the wonder of the place along with his energy. "Just about everything, I guess."

Steele turned and nodded. They started walking toward the house before he spoke. "You've done just fine today. Your help with the direction the investigation needed to head was invaluable." Steele bumped his elbow against Liam's arm. "It's all right, you know."

"What is?"

"Being overwhelmed. I put you in one hell of a position today. The Bureau wanted me to use you as bait. I'm not going to do that. I want your help in this case. Be my partner in this. Tell me what you know, what you've been through, what you assume he's going to do and why. I want you to tell me what you know will and won't work. Together we can get this son of a bitch and keep you safe. Hey… Liam…"

Bait! They were using him to lure Miller back. Lord, he wasn't consulting. He was the carrot. He knew it. He'd be sacrificed to catch Miller. They'd stopped at the front door. Thoughts, questions, and anxiety screamed through his mind. Panic hit hard. Liam clenched his eyes shut. His breath came in small, panting huffs. Terror ripped through the center of his soul and ruptured his thin mirage of control. A rushing, thunderous noise bombarded his ears at the same time his vision tunneled. Liam gasped for air, drowning.

⌒

"WHAT IN THE hell do you mean I should have expected it?"
Steele hissed the retort at Dr. Morgan. Masterson and he had
laid Liam's unconscious form in a bedroom. He'd pulled off
the man's shoes and his jacket, leaving on his jeans and T-
shirt. Steele had piled blankets on top of Liam, hoping to
keep him warm.

"Agent McKenzie, I warned you. I told you how fragile
he was."

Running his hand through his hair for the millionth time
since Liam had passed out, he ground out the words, "What
do I do now?"

"First and foremost, you need to relax. What exactly did
you say to him before he had his panic attack?"

"*That* was a panic attack?"

"From what you described, I'd say yes. Now, what did you
tell him?" The doctor's voice never teetered off pleasant, and
that pissed Steele off. She needed to be more concerned,
because God knew *he* was having a freaking heart attack
right now.

"I told him I wanted to work with him, not use him as
bait like the Bureau wanted."

"I see. And could you see where finding out he was to be
used to entice the man who tortured him for almost two
weeks would be a little overwhelming?"

Steele ground his teeth together. The woman's motherly
'I told you so' tone just had to be right, didn't it?

"What do I need to do to make this better for him? I don't
want to hurt him. Damn it, I feel like I'm kicking a puppy."
Steele fixed his gaze out the window.

"He's not a puppy. He's a man—and a damned good one.
A puppy? Seriously? This man has been stripped of any
defense, used in ways we could only conjure in our worst

nightmares, then recalled by his Bureau to be used, as you so succinctly put it, as bait. When he wakes up, he'll be embarrassed by this event. He'll know you've seen more of his weaknesses. Don't even think about pitying him. He needs support. He knows how to deal with his issues. Talk to him. Let your defenses down so he doesn't feel the need to waste energy on building his. I have a patient waiting. Tell Liam he can call if he needs me."

Okay, so the doctor did have a pissed-off setting, and Steele had just taken a double barrel of it through the chest. He shoved his hand in his pocket. Couldn't she see he was grasping for straws here? The man had scared the shit out of him. One minute Liam was talking with him. The next? Shit, he never wanted to see *that* again.

"All right. Thanks, Doc." Steele ended the call and slipped the phone into his pocket.

"Call me a fucking puppy again and I'll kill you... or myself. I haven't decided which." Liam's soft voice let Steele know the man was awake.

Still looking out the window, Steele wrapped his hand around the back of his neck and sighed.

"If it's any consolation, you're the sexiest puppy I've ever met."

"No consolation, and I don't do puppy play."

"Then you *do* play?"

"Not anymore and stop changing the subject. I don't want your pity."

"Dude, Doc Morgan already ripped me a new asshole for the puppy analogy." He turned back to the room and groaned inwardly. Liam had pushed the blankets off, his lean, muscled body spread across the king-sized bed. A halo of blond hair spread out on the pillow. The man's face flushed with a tinge of rose over his cheeks. His eyes were hooded and heavy. Liam Mercier could quite possibly be the most beautiful man he'd ever seen. The thick full lips flashed a hint of a smile.

"She's good at pulling the rug out from under you. My ass has permanent bruises." A real smile crept out, transforming the man from simmering sensuality to hot-as-fuck.

"Now you tell me? I think we need to work on our communication, especially since we're partners for the foreseeable future." Liam stiffened, the smile vanishing from his mesmerizing brown eyes.

"My preference would be to work with you, Agent McKenzie, but under one condition." Liam sat up, sending his long blond hair to rest on his shoulders. It took everything he had to pull his eyes away from the man's broad shoulders and muscled chest.

"My name is Steele. Partners are on a first-name basis. What is your condition?" He'd give the man any concession to get him on board with his plan.

"When this all heads south, and you know as well as I do that the chances of us catching him before the Bureau demands I be used as bait are next to nothing... give me one thing?"

"Anything." He meant it, too. He'd do, be, say, or work whatever the man needed.

"The respect to tell me I'm Daniel and you're feeding me to the lions. I don't want to be sent to my death without knowing it."

"I'm going to work my ass off to make sure that never happens." Steele's voice cracked from the honest emotion running through him—the emotion he wanted Liam to see and know.

"But when it does. I have to know. I have to prepare or I'll... just promise. I need honesty." Liam's words trailed off.

Steele crossed the room and sat on the bed next to one of the most resilient people he'd had the privilege of meeting.

He extended his hand. "Deal. Complete honesty. The lion clause accepted but hopefully not needed."

Liam looked at Steele's hand and slowly extended his own. The clasp of the man's flesh and inescapable aroma of Liam's blanket-warmed body filled Steele's senses. Desire and need took the form of a metaphoric bullet and shot straight through him.

A soft knock at the door turned Steele's gaze, but not his attention. He held Liam's hand firmly in his, even when Liam tried to pull away.

"Hey, Liam, glad to see you're feeling better. Chief, there is dinner available. The main house's staff were instructed to take care of us for as long as we stay. I think there's enough to feed a small country downstairs."

"Thanks. We'll be down in a minute."

"Agent Masterson? Where's Phil?" Liam tugged at his hand again. Steele released it reluctantly.

"The name is Sam, and he was trailing me a few minutes ago. He's got the run of the place. The house-keeping staff set him up with a litter box and I fed him and gave him water. He's one hell of a cat—or small dog. I'm not sure."

"Thank you for taking care of him."

"No problem. See you downstairs."

Steele chuckled as he stood. "So it's only me the damn thing hates?" He extended his hand and pulled Liam up off the bed.

"Quite possibly." Liam took a hoodie out of his bag and tugged it on, his movements slow and methodical. The man stuffed a medicine bottle in his front pouch and pulled all that long blond hair out of the collar of the warm-up. He'd need more to wear than what he'd brought. Steele made a mental note to get some more warm clothes for him.

Steele bumped Liam's shoulder with his as they exited the

room. "I'll have to work on that. Can't have your pet not liking me."

Steele placed his hand on the small of Liam's back, guiding him through the house.

The tantalizing aroma of food beckoned them to a table that indeed had enough food to feed Luxembourg. Steele heard Liam's stomach growl on the way downstairs. The variety and quality of food passed impressive and kicked remarkable's ass, landing the feast squarely in sumptuous's box. Steele looked up as he grazed off his laden plate and froze. Liam had one small piece of chicken on his plate and wasn't touching that.

Naturally Sam noticed too. "Can I get you something else? The main house has almost anything you'd ever want. Luc is adamant his staff and caretakers keep it stocked at all times." Masterson shortened the rock legend's name as if he'd been doing it for years. How the hell did Sam know Lucifer?

"No, thanks, I'm good. The medicine I take makes my stomach upset and I have to take it on an empty stomach or it won't work well. I don't think you two need to see any more of my little 'events'." Liam made air quotes with his fingers.

"Holy fucking shit!" Steele shouted, and launched off his chair, tipping it over in the process. A streak of flying fur darted out from underneath the table.

"That rat bastard skewered me!" Steele put his leg up on the overturned chair and lifted his slacks, exposing the skin on his shin to his knee. Several small red dots marked his leg. Tiny trickles of blood oozed from the puncture marks.

"Oh my God, you lost your man card for that screech, chief!" Sam's face turned a brilliant red, his deep belly laugh booming through the room.

Liam stood and walked around the table to examine Steele's leg.

"Damn it, Sam, that shit's not funny! I'm going to use that bitch for target practice! I didn't do a damn thing to it and the stealth-mode motherfucker attacked me!" Obviously, Sam had never had four claws full of sharp-as-hell needles jabbed into his leg.

"Oh shit, wait until Fleming and Hardin hear about this. Big, bad-ass team chief taken out by a pussy cat!"

"That isn't a cat! It's the fucking devil!"

Steele tried to hide his smile. He cast a glance at the door where the saber-toothed tiger sat with its tail wrapped around its sheathed, deadly weapons. Blood had to be dripping from his claws. Claws my ass, more like daggers. The rat bastard. He pointed at the cat and made a gun with his hand, miming the motion of shooting the animal. The cat had the audacity to trill at him. Steele faked a lunge toward the damn thing. The cat freaked and tried to gain traction on the hardwood floor as it scurried to get away. Steele righted his chair and sat down, keeping an eye on the door for the freaking ninja-attack-cat-from-hell.

"So Sam, how do you know Lucifer?"

Thank you, little baby Jesus. Liam's question stopped Sam's laughter and pulled his attention away from Steele.

Liam put a small portion of potatoes on his plate and surveyed the rest of the table. Liam missed the look that passed over Sam, but Steele didn't. Whatever the connection between Lucifer and Sam, the history would be interesting to learn.

"Believe it or not, I didn't know who he was when I first met him. He introduced himself as Luc, not his stage name. We spent some time together. I was working a case. We got to know each other."

"Must be a good friend to let us use his house—or rather, one of his houses." Steele egged the conversation further.

"Yeah, he's good people." Masterson slid a glance at Steele

and gave him a nanosecond of a 'fuck-you' look before he cloaked his attitude. Steele took the hint and made a serious attempt at eating his uber-wealthy host out of house and home. But in the end, the food won. Liam ate, but not enough to keep a mosquito alive.

As they left the dining room, Liam swept the damn fur ball into his arms on the way up to his room. The fucking cat had the audacity to purr—or rather, rumble, like a cement truck. The cat gave Steele a conceited and ostentatious glare over Liam's shoulder. Yep, he hated that thing. The rat bastard got to sleep with the world's most beautiful man.

Awesome. I'm jealous of a fucking cat.

CHAPTER 5

*L*iam heard his name called and startled awake. A bare
light bulb dangled precariously close to his face. The
sudden brilliance hurt his eyes and the harsh artifi-
cial glare blinded him. He couldn't blink. His eyes watered.
Tears trailed down the sides of his cheeks and pooled in his
ears. He fought to move, but his body wouldn't respond. *Oh
God! It hurts! Please make it stop!*

"Ah, there you are, my love. My beautiful, beautiful Liam.
It's all right, darling. You're back where you belong. Did you
miss me?"

Miller's face moved into Liam's view. *Oh God!*

"Yes, my lovely man. I see your tears of joy. I know. I
know how happy you are to be back with me. Did you miss
me as much as I missed you? They couldn't keep us apart
after all, could they? I told you I'd come for you, my love.
We'll finish it now, darling. You want me to finish it,
don't you?"

Did he? Did he want it to be over? A release, an escape
from this ledge he balanced on? A chance at peace?

Miller's gloved hand pushed Liam's hair back from his

face. The smell of latex struck a terror so deeply seated in his soul that his heart threatened to explode. And still, he couldn't move.

"It's all right, Liam. You're safe with me." Miller's voice deepened, warped into something else, not the breathless sighed comments he usually used to taunt Liam. Miller advanced with the scalpel.

No! Please, please I want to live! Liam screamed, the plea heard only in his head. He couldn't utter a sound.

Drugged and unable to move, he lay motionless. Once again, Liam was able to comprehend, to feel and to see, but immobile and utterly vulnerable.

Miller's grip on his arm tightened as a gloved hand cupped his cheek. "Liam! It's all right! I've got you."

He struggled to move, but his limbs wouldn't cooperate, the vise-like grip of the drugs holding him frozen and exposed.

Help! Oh God, please someone help me!

～

"LIAM! Wake up. Come on. That's it. It's all right. I've got you. You're safe. You're safe."

Liam jerked hard, trying to pull away. His arms pushed wildly and he grabbed at the hands that cupped his face. No gloves. Not Miller. *Steele.*

Strong, solid warmth enveloped him and Liam dove toward the source. Wrapped securely in Steele's arms, pulled between his muscular thighs, gripped firmly into a hard, muscled chest, Liam burrowed closer. He relished the contact, needed it. The nightmare melted into oblivion and his trembling subsided under the slow, solid pressure of Steele's hands as they traveled up and down his back.

Liam took a deep breath and shuddered, releasing more

tension as Steele's now-familiar scent enveloped him—something profound and rich coupled with a dark spice held together by the unique musk of this man. The heavenly scent replaced the horror of latex. It wasn't Miller. This man, the one holding him, was allowing him to feel, to fear—to be safe. It had been so damn long since he'd felt this warmth. He never thought he'd ever be in a place where he felt safe enough to lie in bed with another man again.

"Do you want to talk about it?" Steele's chest vibrated under his cheek when he spoke.

Liam shook his head and lifted his hand, placing it next to where his cheek lay on Steele's defined chest. The spring of dark chest hair under his hand invited his fingers to feel, to explore. But he didn't. Wouldn't.

The only reason Steele was in his bed now was because of Liam's damn nightmares. His screams. Hell, his own neighbors had called the police when he'd first moved in. His mistake. Now he didn't sleep during the day when his neighbors were out in their yards and might hear.

His fingers crept ever so slightly. The tactile affirmation of the man under his hand caused a shudder to run through him. Tomorrow he'd ask to be taken to a safe house where he wouldn't bother anyone. He'd ask for a guard. Or maybe he'd give Steele whatever information he could and ask to leave—just go home. They wouldn't need him after that. Miller knew Bureau protocol and had made a study of the task force before he'd taken Liam. He attempted to roll away to give Steele the opportunity to leave.

The man shifted slightly but didn't release him. Liam ventured a glance up. Dark blue eyes hooded under long black lashes didn't seem to hold judgment or condemnation.

"I'm not going anywhere. You're safe."

Liam lowered his gaze and shook his head. He wasn't, not

really, although the strength and heat of the man holding him made him long for that feeling.

They lay together, intimate and close, but separated by mountains of emotional baggage. Time slipped past as Steele's hand swept up and down his back in a tender caress. The sensations slowly stilled his frenzied mind. Up and down. Calloused fingertips traced the path, repeatedly. Steele's fingertips changing direction just above the swell of Liam's ass. Never lingering too long, but sweeping slower and lower as the minutes ticked by. Liam's cock thickened against Steele's leg. There was no way he could have stopped his body's reaction to the man holding him, so he didn't try. If Steele was only here for a pity fuck, hell... Liam would take it. He dared to lift his eyes again, breaking the agent's hypnotic caresses. Liam swallowed thickly. No, it wasn't pity he saw, but desire.

Steele leaned into Liam, rolling him onto his back, pinning him to the bed. He pushed his hips down, the movement pressing his thick, hard cock against Liam's leg. God, Liam needed this. Wanted this. He was allowed this, wasn't he? He wasn't an agent and the man wasn't his superior. Steele leaned down, hovering, almost close enough to kiss.

"This is your call. Tell me to stay or to go. We'll only do what you want. No pressure." Another small thrust of Steele's hips accompanied the words. Intentional? Maybe, or maybe Steele needed this as much as he did. Impossible. A man like Steele wouldn't lack for partners. But damn it, even if Liam hadn't been celibate since Miller, he'd want Steele. The man exuded sex from every pore of his body.

Liam gripped the back of Steele's neck and pulled the man down to his lips. The kiss wasn't gentle or sweet. Desperation drove Liam. Steele's body dropped fully on top of him, putting the agent in complete control. Liam's long sleeved T-shirt, sleep pants, and socks disappeared. Steele's hand brushed down the scars etched into his skin and Liam froze.

"Please stop. I… I can't." He pulled away and tried to turn away from Steele. Steele snaked a warm hand around his waist and pulled him back. Skin met skin. Hot, intimate and personal.

"The scars don't bother me, Liam."

"They bother me."

"Let me help."

"How?"

Steele smiled against his skin. "Trust me. Relax for me."

Relax? How in the name of God was he supposed to do that? His breath came in stilted pants. Steele probably couldn't see him well in the darkness, but he could feel what Miller had done.

"I'm here, with you. I'm not going to let anyone or anything hurt you." Steele's whispered words became hot, moist caresses across his collarbone. The soft kisses and lingering touches drove away the fear, the hesitancy.

Liam allowed Steele to lay him flat against the sheets. The man moved, licking, sucking and nipping his way to the hearts and scrolls that trailed from his shoulders down his arms. He tasted, kissed and caressed every inch of the healed incisions. Steele's deft fingers found the raised patterns on his skin, and claimed and possessed each line on his body by tender brushes of his lips and intimate caresses.

Liam groaned with need. He tentatively stroked Steele's back and shoulders. At Steele's encouraging sounds, Liam allowed his hands to discover the hard furrows and plates of muscled flesh above him. He opened his legs, letting Steele settle in between his thighs. Oh, the weight of the man felt so good. Powerful, needy lust reared its head and clawed to escape. This man wanted *him*. And Liam wanted him, too. Oh, God. This…this is real. Warm skin, gentle breaths once again brushed lightly against his neck. The scrape of stubble branded his skin as Steele worked his way across each line of scar tissue, pushing him closer to the edge of coherent thought. Steele expertly maneuvered them both without breaking from the wondrous sensations.

A sudden pull of his nipple into Steele's mouth drew a guttural moan from deep inside Liam. A soft rumbling chuckle sounded, followed by Steele pulling on his tightened nub. Liam bucked against the hard body hovering over him. The feel of Steele's hot, thick, tree-branch of a cock sliding against his own rock-hard dick sent electric pulses through his body. Liam lifted again. The weeping of his pre-cum provided a slick glide that instinctively forced another long thrust. Liam's body shook. This shiver wasn't from the cold. No, Steele's hands touching, his lips exploring, and now, oh God, the rhythmic thrust of his heavy shaft against Liam's were the cause.

Steele used his lips, tongue, and teeth once again to explore Liam's neck and shoulders. Liam pushed his weeping cock up against Steele's prick again, desperate for friction, heat—release. Breathing under the tactile assault ended up as pulled, labored gasps of air as his orgasm built. It wouldn't take much more. It'd been so long and the way their bodies matched perfectly was too good.

Steele used his hand to circle both of their cocks as he claimed Liam's lips. His calloused grip formed the pressure Liam so desperately needed. Liam reached down and wrapped his hand with Steele's, closing the circle of heat and friction. Steele's skin felt velvet soft over the thick shaft. Soft yet so insanely hard. Together they thrust through the tight hold their joined hands formed. The only sounds in the room were their panted breaths, drawn on combined exhales. The overwhelming sensations built, grew sharper and more intense, then exploded as Liam lost it. Hot ropes of semen landed on his stomach as he arched off the bed, lifting the mountain of a man on top of him.

Steele's hot, wet release came seconds later. The man's growled exclamation huffed into Liam's mouth. Panting for air, Liam held the lax weight of the sexy-as-sin man. The heady smell of sex and Steele surrounded him.

Steele lifted up onto his elbow. The rush of cold air onto Liam's chest sent a ripple of shiver across his muscles. Steele dropped a lingering, sweet kiss on his lips and lifted off. Liam watched in shocked silence as the man walked out of the room without glancing back.

~

STEELE GRABBED a washcloth and held it under the tap. He needed to get back to Liam, to ensure he wasn't misunderstanding what had happened between them tonight, or why, because the man would. It was a given. Steele would lay odds Liam was regretting his actions already, and he wasn't going to allow that to happen, for any reason. He wanted more than a hand job with the man. He wanted more... what? Steele stood looking in the mirror, hoping a close up inspection could locate what he actually wanted with Liam, but the blank stare of his reflection apparently didn't have a clue and neither did he. Regardless, he needed to get back to the beautiful man. Steele did a quick splash and wipe, wrung out the hot washcloth, and headed back to the bedroom.

Liam lay curled on his side, the blankets on the bed forgotten in a heap and left on the floor, how they had fallen during his nightmare. Liam fought with desperation when Steele had tried to wake him from the night terror. Liam's blood-curdling screams had torn Steele from a deep sleep. His service weapon now rested on Liam's nightstand where he'd dropped it when Steele realized what was happening. To

keep Liam from injuring himself—or shit, even Steele as he
tried to calm the man—Steele had pretzeled around Liam
and held on tight. Masterson had entered the room right
behind him, but Steele had waved him away as soon as he'd
understood the situation. Liam didn't need more witnesses
to his pain. The man's night terrors had literally become a
vivid and tangible force in the room.

The angelic man curled on the bed had unknowingly
broken each and every good intention Steele had put in place
to keep this situation professional. It wasn't as if Steele had
needed or wanted a relationship. Hook-ups and one-offs had
suited him just fine. Until now. Until Liam. *Fuck it.* Liam
needed him and Steele wanted Liam. Case closed.

He kneeled onto the bed. "Hey, come on. Roll onto your
back. Let me clean you up." Steele placed a hand on Liam's
shoulder. The man jumped under his touch, a strangled noise
escaping him.

Steele clicked on the bedside lamp. In response, Liam
curled farther in on himself in a sharp movement. The scrolls
and heart-shaped scars up the sides of his legs, his arms, and
lining his ribs were a glaring reminder of the torture the man
had experienced.

"Please, turn off the light."

Steele obliged. "Turn over, Liam. Let me take care of you."

"Why?" Liam folded, making himself as small as possible.
The pallor of his skin was a visible hue in the moonlight
seeping through the window.

That was an easy question. "Because I want to."

Steele pulled Liam onto his back and swiped the warm
washcloth over the man's stomach. Liam's hard abdominal
muscle tensed under his touch. So fucking sexy, but those
thoughts shouldn't happen right now. Careful not to linger,
Steele finished wiping their drying cum off Liam and tossed
the cloth into the corner of the room. He reached down and

pulled the covers up before he grabbed at the extra blanket Liam had on the bed and placed it over the man. How he didn't melt into a grease spot under all those layers was beyond Steele.

He eased into the bed and pulled Liam into his side. Tense muscles told him all he needed to know. Well, the man could put up his defenses, but they damn well were having a conversation.

"Now we talk." Steele maneuvered Liam onto his shoulder and started a gentle slide with his hand up and down Liam's arm.

"Talk?"

"Yes."

"About what?"

"What just happened."

"The dream or the sex?"

"Yes."

"Which one?"

"Both."

Liam sighed. The release hadn't lessened the tension in his tightly wound body.

"I have nightmares."

"Obviously. How often?"

A shoulder shrug.

"How often, Liam?"

"Always. They differ in degree. Sometimes I don't wake up. I can sleep through them."

Steele put his fingers under Liam's chin and lifted the man's face. He could see the sad, tired eyes in the moonlit room. "You're telling me you haven't had a peaceful night's sleep in five years?"

"Sometimes I can if I take the drugs."

"All right. Something to work on." Steele ran his hand up and down Liam's arm while his other hand played with the man's luxurious mane of hair. Liam pulled back. The body language told Steele that Liam welcomed the thought of comfort, but his reason for pulling away was yet to be discovered.

"What? You don't want my help?" Steele hooked Liam's leg with his ankle and pulled it in, tangling their limbs together.

"Why would you?"

"Help?"

"Yeah, why?"

Steele reminded himself that both Miller and the FBI had violated, abused and then shunned Liam. The why of the situation? It was fucking obvious he needed help. Reason enough.

"Because I want to."

"It's not that easy." Liam's head moved against his chest. Steele brushed the hair that had fallen over Liam's cheek off his face.

"It *is* that easy. People make things far too difficult. I want to help you, so I will."

"The Bureau won't like this."

"Don't care."

"And that's it? What about your boss? What is he going to say about you adopting a basket case? One the Bureau wants to forget exists?"

"Don't care."

"So it's life according to Steele McKenzie? You do what you want?"

"Within reason."

"And this is within reason?"

"Hell, man, rational thought flew out the fucking window the minute I saw you. But if you're not feeling it, I'll ditch. I don't want to force myself or my help on you." Steele started to lift his arm.

Liam grabbed a hold of him, stopping his movements. "No... stay. Please."

"So this means you enjoyed our time together?" Steele ground out the comment and lowered his head, nuzzling the spot behind Liam's ear. Liam shivered.

"Cold?" Steele grabbed the extra blanket and pulled it up over Liam's shoulder under his chin.

"No. No, I...ahh...it was nice."

"Nice is good." Liam deserved nice. Maybe a little hot and heavy added to spice up the nice.

"Yeah. Nice is something I haven't had a lot of."

"We need to change that."

"He won't let me."

Steele instantly lifted them both into a sitting position. "Hey, that shit stops now. He is not welcome between you and me. Don't give him that power. Understand?"

Liam looked away. His shoulders slumped, defeated. Steele had intended his words to bolster the man. Instead, he'd crushed him. Fuck, he needed to talk to the doc again and get smart on how to relate to Liam, because he would. Come hell or high water, Steele was going to ensure Liam got what he needed.

"I don't know how." The admission exposed a place to start.

"Neither do I, but we'll figure it out."

He pulled Liam down with him again, tucking the smaller man against his side. "I'm here now. Let's try to get some sleep. It'll be a long day tomorrow."

"I'm sorry."

"For what?"

"Waking you. Being... me."

"I have a confession." Steele raked his free hand over his face.

"What?" Liam's body tensed.

"I was jealous of the cat. I'm glad I'm in your bed and he isn't."

Liam chuffed out a lungful of air. "He's not so bad once you get to know him. Give him a chance."

"One more sneak attack and the rat bastard is target practice."

"Everyone gets three strikes. Two more chances."

"Deal. I'd have to buy target ammo anyway. I'm out."

"Trials and tribulations of a federal agent."

"Don't you know it. Now go to sleep."

"Thank you."

Steele brushed a kiss across Liam's brow. The sun rose, casting an orange hue on the walls, before Liam's breath steadied and grew deep. Steele's mind raced over the case, Miller, and what the Bureau wanted him to force Liam to do to attract the attention of a serial killer. If his plan didn't work, he might be compelled to use Liam as bait. But he'd make damn sure the hook he dangled the man on would catch that motherfucker without risking Liam. Somehow.

CHAPTER 6

*L*iam woke instantly. No specter of sleep remained. He knew whose shoulder his head lay on and he remembered every vivid detail of the incredible sex and the strange-as-hell talk Steele had initiated. The agent wanted to help, to be there for Liam. If only it was that simple. The only thing Liam could bring to a relationship was a trans-oceanic freighter full of traumatic issues, phobias and fears. Steele was a good man. Once upon a time, before Liam's world had been shattered, he'd have made a play for the big guy. The dark brown, almost black hair, blue eyes, big muscles, and sexy-as-sin take-charge attitude did it for him. Unfortunately, Miller had escaped and he'd stop at nothing to get to Liam.

But what if Steele was right? Liam froze as his thoughts focused on the alternative. Could they do it? *If* they worked together, *if* Liam fought through the paralyzing fear and gave the team every scrap of information he could remember? He could look at the incoming information. He could help. God, it would be so fucking hard. Liam fought the bile that rose in his throat. The anxiety of just thinking about what he had to do nearly incapacitated him.

But... if they actually found Miller before the lunatic could finish what he started... After all, according to Steele, that was the team's goal—Steele's primary plan. The lead agent was bucking the brass on the 'how' of the plan. That wouldn't go over well once the 'powers that be' found out about the figurative 'fuck you' being flaunted in their direction.

Liam sighed and closed his eyes as the warmth of the agent next to him pulled him into a blissful but short-lived wish for happiness. Right now there was too much standing between Liam and any chance of a happily-ever-after. The largest obstacle was Miller himself. Wrap up the escaped serial killer in Liam's almost incapacitating fears and any chance of a happy ending failed epically.

Liam's eyes popped open. They didn't have much to go on. He could provide some background. After all, they'd accepted his logic and had fallen on the new information about Miller's MO like rabid dogs.

So he'd help. If Steele had been honest in wanting Liam's assistance, he'd do it. Because what happened last night with Steele felt right. For the first time in a very long time, Liam wanted something for himself. He needed the nightmare to end. Oh, he'd always wanted the fear to stop, wanted to feel safe. But now he needed closure for another reason. If he was going to stand a chance at having any type of relationship with Steele, Miller had to be stopped. To stop Miller, Liam needed to face his past.

Liam shifted his legs and stopped immediately as a low rumble started, vibrating the bed. Phil rose from where he'd been sleeping at Liam's feet and stretched into an arch. Liam knew that cat. The arch would recede and soon those sheathed claws would appear as the animal reached forward to knead the bed. Careful not to wake Steele, Liam lifted to chase the feline away before Phil used Steele as a pincushion. Again.

Liam winced at the sharp tug on his hair. Somehow, while they slept, Liam's hair had been pinned under Steele's arm. Phil yawned and reached with his claws.

"No!" Liam hissed at the animal.

"What... huh?" Steele bolted upright, grabbing his gun and Liam in one swift movement. In an instant, he was tight into Steele's side, his face literally smashed against Steele's pectoral muscle.

A flash of brown fur blew past Liam's peripheral vision—Phil, the menace, fleeing the area. Liam was definitely changing his will. Dr. Morgan deserved nothing less than that fur-covered minion from hell.

"Hey, easy." The muffled articulation of his words was a direct result of the precarious face plant and strong arm holding him against some fucking amazing hard chest muscles. Liam placed his hand on Steele's chest in a hesitant hope to reassure the massive man.

It took several seconds before Steele's glare had searched every corner of the room. He eased the safety back on the .45. Liam felt Steele's heavy muscles relax and the gun revert to its perch on the nightstand, but Steele didn't loosen his tight hold. Steele's thundering pulse and staccato breathing resounded around Liam. He tilted his head. His lips grazed the pounding heat under Steele's flesh.

Steele's bed-warmed musky scent enveloped him and Liam wanted nothing more than to kiss the pulse point a millimeter away from his lips. And for once, Liam didn't overthink. He gave in to the urge. Liam pressed his lips lightly against his new lover's warm skin. Steele wrapped his freed gun hand around Liam and he found himself on his back with Steele staring down at him. The fire burning in his gut matched the need Liam saw in those blue eyes.

The feeling of being alive, of being necessary, wanted, even desired, took root deep inside him. He'd do whatever he could to ensure Miller didn't take this from him. He'd rather die than lose this.

"Stop. He doesn't belong here. I want all of your attention and I'm going to be sure I have it."

"You are?" Liam blinked back to the handsome face hovering over him, the words pulling him from inside his own head. He reached up and cupped Steele's cheek with his hand. The rough scratch of the man's thick stubble sent electric trickles through his body. Liam used his thumb to trace the agent's full bottom lip.

Steele trapped Liam's thumb with his lips and pulled it into his mouth. Velvet soft swirls around Liam's trapped digit sent seismic shocks through his body. A flood of blood bloated his already-hard cock. Liam's breath caught. He didn't know how to take in air.

"Mmm hmm." Steele kept his thumb suckled in his soft, warm mouth but smiled, lifting one eyebrow. Liam felt a jolt of desire with that subtle movement.

His lungs expanded. So apparently he could breathe. How? God, who knew? Who cared? He had better things to think about.

"How are you going to do that?" Liam hadn't meant to speak his thought, but he had no control around Steele. Not that he wanted any, which was completely counterintuitive to everything he'd done for the last five years. Releasing his worries and fears, giving them to someone he trusted to protect him, even just for a little while, had once seemed impossible. Now, the need to do just that pushed forward, urgent and unrelenting.

Steele released his thumb, kissing the tip before he responded. "Let me show you."

Liam tensed. An overwhelming need encompassed him. That same desire fought a battle against the fear Miller had planted years ago.

Steele must have felt his reaction. The man's hands cupped Liam's face, tilting it toward his mouth. "I won't force you, baby. This? What we are doing? You decide how far we go. When you want to stop, we will. Okay?"

Steele's warm lips descended and hovered above Liam's as his bold fingers wandered from a feather touch of his cheek to an almost-there brush of his shoulder, teasing and testing. The rough pads of Steele's fingers skimmed down Liam's chest as Steele claimed his lips in a relentless seduction.

Liam grasped the wandering hands and held them, stilling their movements.

"What is it, baby? Tell me what you need. Do you want me to stop?"

Liam closed his eyes and shook his head. No. He didn't want to stop, but he didn't know how to go forward. The specter of his ingrained fear shimmered just beneath the surface, demanding Liam's undivided attention.

Liam licked his dry lips. He watched Steele's dark blue eyes track his tongue's movement. The man lowered his lips, speaking just before flesh met flesh.

"So fucking sexy. Perfect. Beautiful." Steele punctuated each word with a soft brush of his lips against Liam's.

"I'm not." Liam turned his face away from Steele, shielding his eyes from the intense gaze fixed on him from above.

Steele lifted to his knees between Liam's legs, drawing his hands down Liam's body. The touch trailed slowly and brushed the skin nearest his scored reminders of his past.

"You are to me." Steele leaned forward, encircled Liam's

shoulders, and pulled him up against his chest. Steele gripped his hair, tangled the long strands around his fingers, and pulled back, angling Liam's face up. Steele pushed his hips forward, shoving his thick cock against Liam's stomach.

"I want to be inside you someday. Will you let me, angel?" Steele covered Liam's lips with his own in a gentle tender kiss. The sensual assault melted whatever hesitation Liam had thought he had.

"I want that too, but..." Liam held Steele and mapped the hills and valleys of the man's muscled back with his hands, trying to articulate the reason he was hesitant. In a single motion, Steele rolled off Liam, reversing their position. Liam smothered a moan as his weight trapped his cock between them.

Steele pulled him in and sipped kisses from Liam's lips. Liam chased after the gentle, reassuring caresses before his mind engaged. He lifted off Steele, pushing up to his knees, straddling the larger man. His hands traveled as if of their own accord across the defined pecs of Steele's chest. The light dusting of dark hair tickled the palms of his hands as they mapped Steele's contours. Liam lifted his gaze from his hands to meet the lust-filled stare of Steele's dark blue eyes.

Liam moved back until he rested on his elbows between Steele's open thighs. He leaned forward and kissed Steele's hip before he trailed his tongue down the crease between the man's thigh and sex. The man's undeniable musk sent an incredible rush to Liam's deprived senses. Steele's low moan and hand grasping his hair encouraged Liam's exploration.

Liam nuzzled Steele's sack and mouthed him tentatively. Steele's hands applied gentle pressure and his legs dropped even farther. Liam's reserve evaporated. He feasted on Steele's balls, sucking and laving each until the man's thighs trembled. Steele had both hands tangled in Liam's hair and the steady pressure to rise and pay attention to Steele's weeping cock could no longer be denied. Liam ran his tongue from the base of Steele's balls to the tip of his cock, trapping the clear stream of pre-cum that hung in a delicate thread from Steele's uncut cock. Liam paused to run his tongue around the cap, under the foreskin. He couldn't prevent a self-contented smile at Steele's sudden profanity-laced prayer. Steele tightened his large hands almost painfully in his hair before loosening them on a breathless apology. Liam opened his eyes, locking his gaze with Steele's hooded, lust-filled stare, as he took Steele as deeply as he could. Watching the agent's eyes roll back in his head and feeling the man's entire body stiffen ignited Liam's own cock. As he worked Steele's huge shaft farther into his mouth, Liam fucked the bed under him. The delicious friction from the sheets below and the sensory overload of Steele surrounding him set him on a razor-sharp edge.

Steele tightened his hands again and tugged Liam's hair as he spoke. "Close."

Liam moaned and took Steele's thick cock as far as his angle would allow. He hummed his approval of the feel of Steele's shaft thrusting down his throat. Steele's growled curse lingered in the air around them. Liam shuddered as he came at almost the same time. The delicious apex of sensation split his attention, allowing some of Steele's cum to escape. Liam panted hard as he lapped Steele's shaft, cleaning the seed he'd missed.

Steele gently tugged Liam's hair, effectively stopping his admittedly greedy tongue from further stimulating the agent's spent cock. Liam followed the unspoken command and slowly climbed Steele's body before crumbling into an exhausted heap, nestled warmly against Steele's shoulder. The agent caressed the side of Liam's face.

"Fucking perfect, angel. I'll return the favor as soon as I can see." Steele contracted his arm, bringing Liam's entire body into contact with the thick muscles of the man beside him.

"No need." Liam's chuckle preceded his meeting Steele's gaze.

"Really?" That single eyebrow arched again.

"Yeah. Watch the wet spot between your legs." Liam felt the heat rush up his chest and neck. Being fair-skinned, his blushes were almost neon and he knew Steele saw his embarrassment.

"Yeah? That's sexy as fuck. You got us both off with just your mouth." Steele kissed Liam's forehead again. "Talented, sexy, beautiful man."

Liam sighed and closed his eyes. The trifecta of lack of sleep, orgasmic euphoria and body heat from Steele pulled at Liam.

"Go to sleep, angel. I'll watch over you." Content, safe and happy for the moment, Liam registered Steele's words as they seemed to float around him. The unfamiliar caress of contentment pulled Liam away from consciousness.

CHAPTER 7

*L*iam probably wouldn't have been able to convince himself to jog outside if Steele hadn't followed him out of the house and stayed on the porch watching while he exercised. The knowledge the man was there, protecting him, allowed Liam to relax and just run. The feel of his body working hard, the reparative soft thud of his footfall mixed with the cadence of his breath became his only focus. Well, that and the fact his shoes hurt like a bitch. Still, he ran until his raw, blistered feet demanded he stop. He slowed to a walk at the back half of the track he'd used and started back to the house. Steele strolled out to join him, handing him a bottle of water.

"Let's walk a lap and get you cooled down. Do you always go that hard?" They rounded the bend. The backs of three houses looked over the track like silent guardians to the manicured grounds. Shutters cloistered the houses they didn't occupy. Their safe house tucked neatly into the middle lot behind the mansion. Trimmed bushes, steppingstone trails and giant clusters of flowers adorned the area where the track weaved through the grounds. The grounds were beyond beautiful.

"I usually run on my treadmill. I can't... you know, outside... I don't do this well. But all of this? It's amazing." It was hard to admit his weaknesses, even though Steele had seen him at his lowest already.

"It is. But what was different about today? How did you convince yourself to run out here?"

"You came outside and stayed... watching." Liam pulled the elastic out of his hair and allowed it to fall around his face, hiding his blush of embarrassment from Steele.

"That made a difference?" Steele put his hand on the small of Liam's back and slid it around his waist, where he left it.

Liam nodded. "I could have run longer."

"Yeah? Why didn't you?"

Liam looked over at Steele and shrugged. At a gentle nudge of Steele's shoulder against his, he nodded toward his feet. "My feet. These shoes aren't made for running. I didn't bring the right ones. Didn't think I'd be here, doing this."

"Well hell, shoes we can fix. Speaking of being here and doing this, how are you dealing? Are you taking your meds?"

Liam's momentary illusion of normalcy shattered. *The insinuation is that you can fix my shoes but you can't fix me, right?* Liam jerked his chin away from Steele and fought against the flood of self-mutilating anger.

"No. I can't function the way I need to when I'm taking them. Everything is one-dimensional. I can't engage at a gut level. Building this profile for you and your agents... well, I need to be able to give it everything I have."

Steele stopped walking and turned Liam toward him. The man cupped Liam's cheek with his big, warm hand.

Liam leaned into the caress for a moment before he pulled away.

"Not at the cost of your health." Steele's words hurt.

Because I'm damaged goods. "I'll make it. We need an edge. Miller is out there. He's either working out a way to find me or he's going to start taking young men again. I can't let him…" Liam's voice cracked and he dropped his head, trying to keep Steele from seeing his pain.

"Hey, look at me." Steele put a finger under Liam's chin. Instead of fighting it, Liam surrendered to Steele's gentle pressure.

"You don't have to do this alone. If you need anything, I'm there for you. Sam will be with you if I'm not. He'll help too. Okay?"

Liam tried to smile, but the emotion of going through the autopsy files weighed heavy on his shoulders. "I know. This is something I have to do. I have to be able to deal with what he did, not only to me, but also to them. The running helps, but you've got to understand that I *need* to do this. I have to, Steele." He knew his voice sounded tight, desperation tinged with a manic tone.

Steele lowered his mouth to Liam's and kissed him lightly before Liam pulled away. Steele's vivid blue gaze stayed level and direct as he spoke. "I'm here. If you need to run, to talk, or just need me to hold you, I'm here."

~

TWENTY-FOUR HOURS later Liam laced his newly-gifted running shoes—or attempted to. Phil had other ideas. The cat pounced on the neon yellow shoestrings, his rumbling purr squeaked with a hitch as he slapped his paw over the lace that Liam tugged enticingly. The cat was a pain in his ass, but Liam didn't want to think what his life would be like without him. Even with his crazy antics, Liam loved the fur ball. Phil wove himself between Liam's feet and curled around his ankle, ending up on his back, batting at the dangling string like a prizefighter.

The new shoes had been a present from Steele. The agent had bought him a ridiculous amount of clothes and athletic gear. Nobody had ever cared enough about him to spend the time or effort to shop for him. When he was growing up, his clothes were purchased from the thrift store. Waste not, want not. That was his stepmother's belief. And she never wasted a cent on Liam. He'd endured the teasing and taunts from his classmates in school. The patches in his jeans and the ill-fitting shoes and coats made him even more awkward than a typical teen.

Tall, too thin, and introverted, Liam had struggled to fit in, and that was without anyone knowing he was gay. He had no friends and spent the majority of his time studying. During his mandatory guidance counseling session when he was a freshman, his advisor had told him that if his grades were good enough, he could earn a scholarship to go to college. The woman seemed to understand his misery. She pulled him into her office every chance she could and had encouraged his studies. She even helped him apply for grants and scholarships. He wouldn't have been able to escape his life without that woman.

He'd worked a part-time job since he was fourteen. He was paid under the table and the majority went to his parents, but he squirreled away enough to buy some basic clothes when he left for college. Liam had almost choked at the price tags that hung off the clothes in the bags, until Steele told him he was expensing the purchase. The man had said he figured the FBI owed Liam new clothes. The name brand items definitely didn't come from the second-hand store.

Phil tired of chasing the shoestring and wandered over to a slice of sunshine on the floor. His Majesty stretched out in the light and closed his eyes. Content and purring, Phil summarily dismissed Liam, so he strung the eyelets of his new running shoes before he made his way down the stairs. He'd been working the autopsy reports, mining the information for anything that would help him fill out the ritual of Miller's kills. Miller's sadism forced the memory of Liam's own violation front and center. Today, like yesterday, he ran to exorcise the horror from his mind. Complete and utter exhaustion quieted his demons—sometimes.

The visuals of the autopsy pictures, however, were fucking with him. He swallowed hard and forced his focus away from the pain the words and photos dredged up. The need to escape pushed him outside to the track again. Liam waited for Steele to walk out to the porch before he dropped off and started out at a slow jog. His very expensive running shoes eased his sore, tired feet. His body warmed after the first quarter mile. Liam pumped up his pace—a desperate effort to escape the demons. He ran until the pictures and voices of the past didn't exist. And it helped... for a while.

≈

"Taking a break?" Steele glanced up at Masterson's words. He lifted his chin toward Liam. The man flew across the mile-long running path that circled the tennis courts and wove in between the first and third holes of the golf course behind the house they were using. Every day without fail, when the information in the folders became too much, Liam would run like the hounds of hell were chasing him—and perhaps they were. Steele made sure he stayed where Liam could see him. Since the first day when Liam had told him that the fact he watched helped to calm Liam's fears, he'd made it a point to be present. That alone made this time away from the case they worked important, even though he hated watching the man pound himself into the ground.

"If he can see me, he feels better. He's working without a safety net. He stopped taking his meds so he could concentrate."

"He's a tough man, boss. You're falling for him."

"I'm just trying to take care of him. He didn't ask for this. We forced him into it." Who the hell was he trying to fool? He'd fallen. Process the scene. The evidence would convict him.

"True. But you *are* falling down a rabbit hole, chief. I've seen it. Lived it. A word of advice? Make sure you can do what's best for him, even if it means letting him go and walking away. When people are hurt as badly as he has been... well... they need, almost desperately, and they can become your entire world when they're recovering, but sooner or later, they need to stand and fly on their own. If you're lucky, he'll come back."

"You weren't lucky, were you?"

Masterson's eyes held a faraway look. A small smile tilted the corners of his mouth. "Ahh... well, I guess, yes and no. It's a double-edged sword. He's healthy and thriving and that's a good thing. I haven't seen him in a couple of years. I've invented reasons not to be where he is so he'd be able to focus on what he needed to do. We've exchanged a few emails, texts, and a call or two. I keep tabs on him. He's healthy and happy; knowing that keeps me somewhat sane."

"That's why you haven't been with anyone long term?" As long as Steele had known Masterson, the man had only done one-offs. Masterson had never hit him as the relationship type. The man took what he needed and left. He'd never suspected Sam was hung up on someone.

"Yeah."

"He's a fool. How could he leave you knowing how you felt?"

Sam squirmed in his deck chair and reached for his soda.

"Ah hell, Sam. You didn't tell him how you felt?" Steele tried to wrap his head around that revelation.

Masterson gave a careless shrug that anyone else might have bought. Steele didn't. "He's better off without me holding him back. And with that, I'm done talking about it. Just be careful, chief. I don't want you to get hurt." Masterson took a drink of the cola he held.

"You going to tell me who?"

"No." A determined shake of Sam's head accompanied his comment.

"I could find out." It might take a hot minute, but he'd be able to figure it out.

Masterson's eyes narrowed as they sliced toward Steele. "You won't, though."

"Don't like not knowing." Which was why he'd become an investigator.

"Don't care."

"Noted."

"Noted? Please, don't fucking push on this, chief. It's personal." The passion in Masterson's voice made the comment harsher than the man had probably intended.

"He deserves to know." Hell, he'd want to know, wouldn't he?

"Nah, he's happy."

"How do you know?"

Sam drew a deep breath and tapped the outside of his sweating soda can with his fingers. Movement to the right caught their attention and they watched as Liam flew past. The pace the man maintained would grind Steele's ass into the ground. And he'd done exactly that yesterday when

Steele had made the mistake of thinking he could keep up. Lesson learned. His legs still fucking hated him.

Finally, Sam responded, "Same way you know when Liam is upset. I've seen you reach out and touch his arm without looking up from your work. You can sense when he needs grounding. You have a connection."

"True. I won't deny that." Really, how could he? The connection he shared with Liam was freaky intense. But what was between them also felt comfortable, effortless, and right.

"Tell me honestly that you wouldn't walk away if you knew Liam would be better off, healthy and happy, without you. You can't, can you? Hell, chief, I knew I wasn't what he needed. It doesn't make me love him less." Sam stood and nodded toward the house. "So how about I go back and get after what I get paid for?"

"Avoidance maneuver?"

"Done sharing."

"Copy that." Steele locked onto Liam as he rounded the corner near the first tee. Could he walk away from Liam? Steele shook his head. *No.* There was no way in hell he could be that selfless. He'd stay and fight.

CHAPTER 8

"*A*lthough we know nothing is guaranteed with psychotic killers, we do know Miller is ritualistic and obsessive-compulsive. The room he'll set up will be cleared in the right hand corner, closest to the door. This area is his safety zone, where he thinks. This is what he calls his vision field. It's where he creates his artistry and how he focuses his energy. If you have him located and move on him, that is the first place to look. When he is threatened or think-ing, this is his safety, his security."

The team agents were taking notes as he spoke. After days of working to trace possible routes, locations, and leads on Miller, the team had taken a break from sifting through mountains of information. The intrinsic data he now provided hadn't been presented to anyone before. Hopefully, it would help. If nothing else, forcing himself to look at Miller as a subject rather than his tormentor had made the killer more... human? No, perhaps less demonic would be a better descriptor.

Liam shook off his exhaustion and wandering thoughts and focused on completing his commentary. "These boards represent the abduction he processes his victims through. By coroners' and doctors' reports, we know each victim is treated the same, each endures the process on these boards. According to the autopsy reports I've gone through, with the exception of me... N-n-none, ahh..."

Bile rose from his gut and burned in the back of his throat. He drew shallow breaths and continued, "None have made it past day eleven. Those who died were lucky." His last words were whispered, almost to himself.

Liam cleared his throat to try to assuage the swelling ache of emotions. Without his anti-anxiety meds, going through the autopsy reports had successfully balled up every last memory of those horrible days and shoved them down his throat. *Less demonic? Not a fucking chance.*

With a start, Liam realized he'd stopped talking. *Damn.* Abruptly facing the board, he continued his narration. "He starves and denies the victim water for days while making each victim learn a ritualistic bathing sequence. They're forced to use rubbing alcohol to perform the ablutions, not water. If the victim does not comply, Miller electrocutes him through a charge he sends via the metal grating the prisoner stands on. The shock is not enough to kill—as long as the victim does not have any health issues. According to autopsy reports, victims number three and nine died by heart failure, probably during this phase. Electrical shock is extremely useful in motivating the victim to do what he wants. The voltage is increased until compliance—or death—is achieved. At this point in the process, Miller has no artistic effort invested in the victim. He doesn't care one way or the other if his victim lives or dies. Unfortunately for the victim, the human will to survive is stronger than most would believe."

Liam closed his eyes, trying to stave off the panic attack that thrummed just below the surface of the façade he attempted to project. The overwhelming fear was there—surging, ready to overrule his ability to cope.

His stomach rolled violently as bile once again backed into his throat. *Help me do this, God. Please, give me the strength.* Swallowing with effort, he cleared his throat and continued. "Anyway… the victim has been without drinking water for days, so in order to survive, he will drink whatever Miller gives him. The water is drugged, and when they succumb, they are moved into his art studio. This is where Miller's IV concoction of drugs is administered. There were several theories as to what combination he uses. Regardless, the cocktail freezes the muscles of the body but leaves the mind completely awake."

∿

LIAM STOOD at the board looking ghostly pale but obviously not seeing the words he had written. Black circles under his expressive brown eyes, the slump of his shoulders and sluggish movements showed just how depleted the man had let himself become. Liam's voice trailed off. Steele moved away from the wall, drawing Liam's attention. A faint lift of his lip flickered before Liam turned away from the board and continued, "The victim knows what is happening. They are alert and conscious, and they feel everything. *Everything.* But they can't move or scream. Day five is the first day of 'artistic treatment'."

Steele moved closer when he noticed Liam's breaths had reduced to shallow pants and the pallor of his face flushed out even farther.

"The day begins with Miller transferring the victim from the floor of the cell to his art studio. He… manages the victim. Catheter, enema, IV… drugs…"

Steele reached the front of the room.

Liam stared through him as he spoke. "The victim stays 'attached and on display' from that point forward. Miller considers himself an artist. Each day he carves into a different portion of the victim. First, he'll wash them with rubbing alcohol because after day five the victim cannot move on his own. The studio, as he calls it, is cold... so damn cold." Liam wrapped his arms around himself.

Steele moved closer and placed a hand at the small of Liam's back. He and his team waited for several minutes before Liam moved. Evidently the man had gone somewhere in his head. Liam once again shook out of the memory and glanced up in surprise at Steele.

Liam cut a quick glance to the agents gathered in the room before he turned and spoke directly to Steele, as if the other people present didn't exist. "He told me while he was carving that the cold keeps the blood loss to a minimum. Miller detests anything getting in the way when he's carving. He wipes the blood away with rubbing alcohol pads so his vision is unimpeded. After a while, the pain is indescribable. Miller monitors the victim's heart rate and blood pressure. Should it elevate to a dangerous level, he'll stop to soothe the victim... promises he's almost done for the day. He'll wait... then start the process again."

Liam waved half-heartedly at the boards he'd set up in the library of the house they'd continued to use. "As noted, each day a different portion of the victim's body is 'enhanced' until he reaches day thirteen. This day is the first day the art is worthy of his..." Liam visibly shuddered and drew his arms tightly against himself. "His display equipment is built to hold the drugged victims while he..." Liam's voice cracked and a single tear slid down the side of his cheek. He stood quietly facing the board representing the torture of day thirteen.

Steele took over. Liam had walked him through his

briefing before his agents had gotten there. He wanted a dry run to ensure he could handle the mental challenge. Steele now knew the unadulterated truth of what Liam had lived through. If Steele ever got within a half-mile of that bastard Miller, he'd make sure the man wouldn't have any opportunity to hurt another soul.

Steele picked up the briefing, trying to bring it to a succinct ending. "This is for your information. No other people in the world know about this. It wasn't disclosed to the Bureau. As far as we know, they didn't ask, neither did the courts."

Eyes downcast, Liam walked out of the room. Steele knew what the briefing had cost the man. He needed to get upstairs to catch Liam before he crashed.

"Commit this information to memory. It is our edge and our timeline if or when that bastard strikes. Work the hospitals. This type of medical equipment has to be accounted for in some fashion. Get inventories, contact hospital administrators, and have them run every piece of this equipment they own to the ground. Get ahold of the national HIPAA gurus and have them threaten an audit if the administrators balk. That will force them to comply. Hands-on accountability, I don't want some slacker to assume something is there that isn't. Put pressure on them and keep it on until we know for a fact that they aren't missing anything. Hit up medical supply companies and warehouses and do the same. Scour those energy consumption reports. Work in quadrants along the most expeditious escape routes, and work fast. All data from the locals and from our other avenues of intelligence need to be bumped against each other. We have authorization to pull more people in to do the grunt work if we need them. Sam, you've got point till I get back. Get ahold of the people you need and get them started, but don't bring them here. We need to stay off the grid."

"Chief? How in the fuck did he live through it?" Hardin threw his chin in the direction Liam had gone. The question echoed in the large room.

Steele paused on his way out the door. He looked back over his shoulder. "He's a survivor and he's strong. Regardless, if we don't get Miller soon, they're going to force me to use him as bait. I need your help to make sure that doesn't happen. Please." He looked straight into the eyes of each of his agents before he hit the stairs. They were onboard and he needed to be elsewhere.

Steele pounded up the staircase. Worry tore at him. For the last four days, Liam had been withdrawn. He'd claimed it was a side effect of going off his medication, but in his gut, Steele knew better. Since their first morning together, Liam hadn't slept more than a handful of hours and barely talked, other than short replies to direct questions. The man literally ran himself into the ground. The intensity of facing what Miller had done, not only to him, but to each of his victims, nearly consumed Liam. Running seemed to help him cope, but without proper sleep and food, Steele honestly didn't know how much longer Liam could go on.

When Steele tried to comfort him, he'd pulled away, become distant. Doc Morgan said it was a typical response to the stress. She'd held extra sessions with Liam to help him cope with the memories the autopsy reports had dredged up. She'd told Steele that giving the briefing would be a big milestone in his recovery.

Steele wouldn't classify the briefing today as big. Massive, gigantic, or colossal, perhaps. Big didn't hold a candle to what Liam was dealing with right now. Alone.

Steele knuckled Liam's bedroom door, opening it without waiting. The room was empty but the sound of the shower drew Steele toward the en suite bath. Steam billowed out as Steele moved in.

Liam stood naked beside the shower. Silver and red scars decorated his body in a sick twist of ivy and heart scroll-work. Seeing the scars in the daylight and in their entirety filled Steele with anguish and rage.

"This is what he did." Liam focused on the falling water.

"I know."

"He took my dignity, my sense of safety. He raped me, physically and mentally. The others didn't live. He told me I was his special gift from God. He believes we are meant to be together for eternity. He won't stop. He'll come for me." Liam lifted his gaze and Steele witnessed the devastation held in the chocolate-brown depths. "By the time they deciphered my notes and found me, I'd given up. I wanted Miller. When he... I wanted to please him, to be good enough for him so he'd stop the pain. I wanted to be what he said I was." Liam's voice broke into a sob.

Steele shut the bathroom door and stripped out of his suit, placing his automatic on top of the hurriedly shed clothes before he crossed the room. His hand fell on Liam's shoulder, but the anguished man didn't move or acknowledge the touch. "Liam, let me help." Steele brought his chest to Liam's back and peppered his shoulders with quick, light kisses.

Liam closed his eyes and nodded his head. A slow, fat tear trickled down his cheek.

Steele continued pouring attention on the man. "Do you know what you are?"

"An abomination. A sick, twisted abomination." Another tear dropped, traveling the same path.

Steele paused at the comment. Why would Liam think he was the abomination? Miller was the fucking animal. He turned the shattered man toward the bathroom's full-length mirrored wall. "No, you're a survivor. Open your eyes, angel."

Liam opened his eyes and winced at the reflection. Steele slid both arms around Liam's waist. He belted the shorter man to his body with one arm and snaked the other up his chest, lightly grasping Liam's jaw. He leaned forward and whispered in his ear. "You're strong. So damn strong, babe. You did what you had to do to survive. The man you have trapped in your memory isn't the man I see. You are neither his creation nor his exhibit. You are bruised and a little broken, but you are so much more than what he did to you."

"I'm not. How can you say that? How can you even touch me?" The anguish and sorrow behind the question nearly floored Steele.

"Because I see *you*, not what he did to you. You are an amazing man. Dedicated, caring, and so damn strong. When we were together I saw the hot flush of arousal build over your chest and creep up you neck. I saw your eyes darken into the most intense shade of brown, so dark with desire that they're almost black. And that mouth... fuck, you are my dreams come true."

Steele traced Liam's plump bottom lip with his finger. He watched Liam's eyes track his movements in the mirror. "When you came that night, you bit your bottom lip to stop your moan. It was the sexiest fucking thing I've ever seen. I want more of the hot-as-fuck man in front of me. I want to feel this hair fall over us when you ride my cock. These muscles?" Steele moved his confining arm up and traced the clearly visible ridges of Liam's defined abs. "I want to watch them clench and roll with desire. I see a man who is alive, sexy, and strong. I see a man who I'd be honored to call mine. I see *you*, Liam, not what was done to you, not what was left on your skin. I see *you* and I want *you*. So. Damn. Bad." Steele punctuated the last three words with kisses along Liam's neck.

Liam met his gaze in the mirror. "You want me even after you know what he did?"

Steele held the look and told the unadulterated truth that Liam needed—no, deserved to hear. "I don't care what he did. I know that's crass, and I don't say it in an attempt to belittle what happened, but the things that were done to you have zero bearing on how I feel about you. I want you, Liam, with scars or without scars. The marks, physical or emotional, don't matter to me. *You* matter." Steele dipped his head, his lips finding a spot behind Liam's ear. A shiver ran through his man, and this time Steele knew it wasn't from the cold.

"I want to take care of you. Let me. You have to be exhausted."

"So tired." A whispered agreement.

"I'll take care of you tonight, angel."

Steele turned Liam and pulled the shorter man into the shower. "Put your hands on the shower wall."

Steele positioned the showerhead and poured a palm-full of body wash as Liam placed his hands on the tile. Steele moved, carefully continuing the sensual touches that slathered Liam's back in slick foam. Liam's muscles tightened and clenched, hard under Steele's hands.

Steele dug his fingers into the tired ropes of sinew and slowly kneaded the tense knots in Liam's shoulders and upper back. With a quiet determination he worked lower as, little by little, Liam's muscles started to relax. Steele focused on the small of Liam's back. The muffled sob he heard validated his gut instincts. The poor man hadn't been cared for in so damn long that he'd forgotten how to relax and let someone else help him, if only for a short time.

Steele dropped his hands to Liam's glutes and worked those tight, hard globes of flesh. Any other time he'd take a detour and sweep a finger into the warmth of the man, but right now, it wasn't sexual. This was just basic human contact. Steele worked over Liam's entire body. He gave everything he could to the exhausted man through his touch and proximity. Trembling from the ministrations, Liam slowly melted forward, ending with his cheek pushed up against the marble tile of the shower wall. Steele smiled as he lowered to his knees and worked down each leg, rubbing, touching, and soothing tired, needy muscles.

Steele rinsed both of them off and poured a good amount of shampoo into his hand. He washed the abundance of long, blond hair. He'd never thought he'd be attracted to a man with long hair, but on Liam, the effect was drop-your-pants sexy. He worked the soap through, then started massaging Liam's scalp. What was left of the man's tension melted. If there was a part of Liam's body that wasn't relaxed, it wasn't from Steele's lack of effort. He adjusted the spray of the showerhead to ensure all the soap was out of Liam's long blond locks before he shut off the water.

Grabbing a couple of towels, Steele dried Liam's hair and wiped him down gently. With a quick swipe over his own skin, he grabbed his stack of discarded clothes, along with his gun, before leading the quiet and relaxed man into the bedroom.

Steele stutter-stepped when he caught a movement at the foot of the bed. Phil trilled softly and Steele may have growled. The damn stealth-mode, ninja-wannabe, mother-fucking cat wasn't going to stop him from taking care of Liam. Determination won over the spike of adrenaline Phil induced, because it wasn't fear. Nope, he was not afraid of the fur ball. At all. If the rat bastard so much as hissed at him, he'd dropkick it or shoot it—if he could catch it. The vermin was surprisingly fast.

Thankfully, Phil stood, stretched in a magnificent arch, and wandered to the far side of the bed, where he curled into a ball and blinked at Steele. Keeping an eye on the demon from hell, Steele dropped his clothes next to the bed, put his gun on the nightstand, and pulled the blankets down. He took Liam's towel and helped him slide between the sheets. Steele followed the shower-warmed man into folds of soft Egyptian cotton. Cool strands of damp hair licked across Steele's chest as he settled Liam into position tucked tightly against his shoulder.

"Thank you." Liam's whisper came out as barely a breath of noise.

"You're welcome." He pressed his lips to Liam's freshly-shampooed hair. The even, gentle pulls of air told him the man in his arms was close to falling asleep. Steele cast an eye down toward the cat. The animal's yellow eyes stared unblinking, and Steele was damned if he'd be the first to look away. Finally, the cat blinked and lowered its head, tucking into a ball. The room filled with a low rumble. Steele smiled as he ran his hand through Liam's drying hair. If he could, he'd purr like that damn cat too.

"Steele?" Liam's hips pushed forward slightly. Liam's hot cock pressed against Steele's hip.

"Need something?"

Liam nodded. His hand drifted across Steele's chest, lightly grazing his nipples. A shot of electricity zapped down his body and pooled at the base of his spine.

"What do you need?" Steele continued to run his fingers through Liam's hair.

"Make me forget him." Liam's soft plea would have landed Steele on his ass if he hadn't already been lying down.

Steele's cock could have cut diamonds. He was that hard. But his need didn't matter. Liam's did. Steele's hand trembled as he reached out and cupped Liam's neck, pulling him closer. He brushed Liam's lips with his. "I can do that."

Steele lifted over Liam. He mapped Liam's chest and

shoulders with his hands and lips. He nipped the skin at the base of his throat and sucked it into his mouth, pulling the blood to the surface. The way Liam's body arched into his and the low groan that accompanied his efforts gave Steele a nugget of information to work with. He added strength to his grip and turned his light caresses into points of possession. Liam's verbal and physical response was a thing of beauty. He pushed into Steele's rougher, heavy-handed seduction and moaned. His man liked to know he was being claimed. Liam wanted to forget, to ride a wave of something good. Reading Liam's responses to his growing aggressiveness, Steele knew how to make that happen. With a single purpose in mind, Steele unlatched the cage he'd wound around his own desires.

Steele worked his way down Liam's body, devouring, exploring and claiming. His lover's pale skin marked beautifully. Steele proclaimed his possession of Liam with a trail of light bites as his tongue, lips and teeth left their lust-driven marks on Liam.

Steele kissed Liam's hipbone and flicked his tongue across the very tip of Liam's weeping cock. Liam's fair skin showcased the dark blue veins that fed his well-proportioned shaft. Absolutely everything about this man was beautiful.

"Such a pretty cock, Liam." Steele anchored Liam's rock-hard dick into his hand and fisted it hard, pulling a stroke up to the tip before he twisted his hand and lowered to the base again. Liam's body tensed and arched into Steele's grasp.

"Ahh, so good. Don't stop, please."

"I'm not stopping." As if to prove his statement, Steele dragged his hand up Liam's weeping shaft again. Copious amounts of pre-cum lubricated the slide. Steele cupped Liam's lightly furred balls in his hands and pulled slightly. Liam's response was immediate and devastatingly needy.

"I want to be inside you, Liam. But I'm willing to let you

take whatever it is you need. How do you want this to play out, baby?" Steele had bottomed a total of once in his life and the experience hadn't been pleasant, but he'd gladly give himself to Liam if that was what the man needed.

"No… I need you in me. I need you to make him go away. He… he was the last. I don't want him to have that… me, anymore."

Steele dropped back over his man and grabbed his face with both hands. "I'm going to take you, angel. Unless you tell me there is a reason we shouldn't do it bareback, I'm going to fuck you hard and leave my cum inside you. Take you and mark you as mine. He doesn't have you anymore. I do. Do you understand? You're mine."

Liam's eyes pleaded as he spoke. "I'm negative. I was tested after… I trust you if you say you are. Please, just make me forget what he did."

Steele dove down and captured the man's mouth. The tenderness was gone. He was claiming what was his and driving the phantom of Miller away from Liam. Steele took control of the kiss, using his grip on Liam's hair to angle him for deeper access. When he broke it, Liam's eyes had lost focus. Steele smiled and licked at Liam's lips before he once again traveled the length of pale, smooth skin. He could worship Liam's body until eternity ended and still not get enough of the man.

Steele kissed the hot, dark red tip of Liam's cockhead. Liam repeatedly gripped the sheets, his low moans and panting breaths a symphony of desire and need. Steele reached up and tapped Liam's lips with his fingers. "Get them wet, angel."

Liam swallowed Steele's fingers as Steele dropped over Liam's cock and took it into his mouth, teasing the sensitive underside before he swallowed the man to the back of his throat. Liam's tongue stopped its movement over Steele's fingers and he moaned, bucked up and tensed. Steele circled the base of Liam's cock with his free hand squeezing as he lifted away.

"Oh, that was close. I'm not letting you come until I get inside you. I want to feel you around me when you do."

"Please. Please, I need..." Liam repeated the words in a whispered chant.

"I got you. I'll give you everything you need, baby."

Steele used his shoulders to push Liam's legs open farther. "Hold your legs back." If he didn't get the man opened up soon, he could kiss any chance of penetration good-bye. Just the feel of Liam's tongue around his fingers brought him to the edge of sanity.

The vision of Liam pleading and spread open for him now was almost too much, but Steele forced himself to take in every aspect of the beautiful man. The picture of Liam undone and under him was a memory he wanted to get right, to be able to recall for a lifetime. Because this man was a once-in-a-lifetime gift, someone to be cherished, cared for, and loved. Steele swallowed hard at the thought. He traveled his moistened fingers across the sensitive skin below Liam's tight, full balls before he circled the small pucker of pink skin, exploring and teasing. Steele glanced at Liam and froze as he locked gazes with the chocolate-eyed lust-filled stare.

"Lube." Liam's comment amused Steele. He lifted an eyebrow and gave the guy a half smile and nodded toward the side of the bed.

"Wallet. Suit jacket." Liam scrambled to the edge of the bed and grabbed Steele's wallet, tossing it to him as he scooted back to his original position.

"In a hurry?"

"Fuck yes." Liam panted the words. He grabbed his cock and stroked it, watching Steele. Liam grazed over his own nipple, and he pinched the nub, sucking in air and closing his eyes with a low mewl.

"Oh, holy fuck, Liam. You're one sexy bastard." Steele pulled a small packet of lube out of his wallet. He tore the foil and squeezed half out in a line between his index and middle finger. He bent over Liam, holding himself up with one arm. Lowering himself, he lubed the smaller man's entrance. He smiled when Liam gasped and opened his eyes.

"Oh." Liam's surprised whisper escaped just as Steele's finger breached the tight muscle.

"Yeah, baby, you're tight. I'll go slow. Open you up. Make you want me." Steele dipped down for a lingering kiss. He pressed kisses into the man's jaw, neck, and chest. He added a second finger as he lapped at the light golden treasure trail until Liam's cock bumped his chin. Steele teased Liam, never quite giving him enough. Steele worked a third finger inside Liam, scissoring the man's tight channel to loosen and relax the clenching muscle. Steele rotated his hand and searched until he found the small gland. His lover's body jerked at the first brush over his prostate. Liam arched and shouted at Steele's repeated touch. Steele gritted his teeth as Liam pushed against his hand, fucking himself on Steele's fingers. *Sexy bastard.*

"Steele… gonna…" Liam grasped at Steele's arms.

Steele pulled his fingers out of Liam's body and circled the base of his cock once again, adding enough pressure to help stave off the orgasm. "Shhh… not going to come until I let you."

"No, please… please don't stop!"

The pride-filled internal roar of his dominant male threatened to erupt. He could edge the man like this for hours; make him lose his mind in sensation. Actually, a long edging session was just the thing to wipe Miller from Liam's mind. Steele placed a calming hand on Liam's stomach. "I'm not stopping, baby. Let go. Trust me and I'll make you forget everything."

Liam's body relaxed under him and Steele exhaled at his response. Liam trusted him, and he'd make sure that trust was safeguarded, protected, and cherished. He layered his words of praise with possessive touches. Steele's attention focused on Liam, and he became acutely attuned to the man under him. Time and his own need ceased to exist. Steele pushed Liam to the very brink again, and again, ignoring his pleas for release. When Liam finally surrendered and stopped trying to control the experience, Steele gave a mental fist pump. Liam's responses smoothed, his moans and panting breaths became subdued, a background to what Steele's hands and mouth were doing to his body. The man rode the rising wave that Steele's skilled fingers and mouth created. Steele spread the remaining lube on his cock and centered himself on Liam.

Steele leaned over and sipped several kisses from Liam's lips. "Open your eyes for me, angel."

Liam fluttered his long dark-blond eyelashes open, exposing pupils that were blown wide with lust, leaving only the smallest ring of dark chocolate brown visible. At that moment, Steele knew Liam was floating somewhere between ecstasy and torment, riding the intense sensations Steele was forcing his body to endure.

"Are you ready, baby? Do you want me inside you?"

"Please." A single tear trailed out of the corner of Liam's eye.

Steele kissed the salty drop from Liam's temple as he pushed into him. Liam's guardian muscle stretched tightly over Steele's cockhead.

"So good, angel. Bear down, baby. I don't want to hurt you." Steele panted, waiting to feel the response to his words. Liam's body complied and Steele pushed inside his man.

Heat and the insanely tight grip of Liam's body instantly demanded Steele stop moving. If he didn't, he'd hurt Liam, and Steele would be damned if he'd ever allow that to happen.

Liam gripped Steele's biceps in a crushing grasp. The bite of pain only added to the need to lurch back and thrust deep into the extraordinary man under him. Steele hung his head and gritted his teeth, begging every deity he'd ever heard of for control. Sweat trickled down Steele's back and time stopped until Liam let out a slow breath and loosened his grip.

"Move. Please, move now." Liam's panted plea was a blessed answer to his prayers. Lying with Liam's legs wrapped around him, he did just that. Steele released a long, slow breath as he withdrew. He lowered his lips and inhaled Liam's exhaled breath. Their eyes met and held, engulfed by an emotion so deep Steele couldn't understand it, one that reared its head and consumed him. A shudder of pure sensation rushed through his body when he felt Liam's body clench around his cock, wrapping every nerve ending in tantalizing friction. Steele halted before he pulled free and made the return thrust with slow, languid intent. He hit Liam's prostate. The response—a sudden lurch and moan from the man under him—only intensified the need to withdraw and thrust again. Steele kept the deliberate, measured pace, slowly driving himself and Liam toward the edge. This time, he'd let Liam step off the cliff, but he'd be there to catch him.

Liam gripped at Steele's back and lifted his hips, meeting each thrust of Steele's cock. Steele held Liam close. Cheek-to-cheek, their panted breaths fanned heated skin, a slow scintillating merging of bodies. Liam cupped Steele's face, pulling him back for another kiss.

Liam whispered, "I'm coming," just before his body tightened and his back arched. A warm wet sensation pooled between their sweat-slicked bodies as Steele's cock exploded in the vise-like grip of Liam's clenching depths. His hips thrust and he spilled deep inside of Liam, then collapsed against the defined chest below him.

Once he'd caught his breath, Steele rolled off Liam. He turned his head, whispering against Liam's ear, "That was beyond anything I've ever experienced before. You are amazing."

"I never knew it could be so... damn." Liam turned to his side, facing Steele.

"Yeah, usually isn't. Not for me, at least. That was..." Steele had jumped in head first and, of course, into the deep end of whatever emotion he was feeling. He'd had plenty of sex, but this? Fuck, this wasn't sex. Well, it was, but it was so much more than just that.

"Hot?" Liam guessed.

"God, kind of more than that, wasn't it?" Steele tried to find the words.

"Insane, intense, mind-blowing, write an article for Penthouse good?" Liam's eyebrows rose at his question.

"Yeah, all of that too. You're screwed now... you realize that, right?"

Liam laughed, a deep belly laugh that rolled around the room. "I believe I was very well screwed, thank you very much." The happiness in his eyes was something Steele would kill to keep there.

"Yeah, well... you're welcome. But I meant you're screwed because you aren't going to get rid of me now."

Liam closed his eyes, but the soft smile on his face remained. "Maybe I'd be okay with that. If you can deal with my baggage."

Steele leaned forward and kissed Liam's temple. "The good thing about baggage is that it can be unpacked and put away. It's temporary." Steele kissed the blond hair again. "I'll go get a towel to clean you up."

Liam's tired hum drew a satisfied smile. Steele was exhausted, and he hadn't had the emotional turmoil Liam had faced. The man had to be drained. Steele made quick work of cleaning up and returned to take care of his lover. His... lover. *Damn.*

CHAPTER 9

The soft ache of his body when he turned in bed put a smile on Liam's face. He felt used, but in the most wonderful way. He could feel Steele's warmth next to him and he pushed a little closer to the man. He radiated heat like a furnace. Liam took a deep, cleansing breath and opened his eyes. The sun was already high in the sky. A sense of wonderment hit him. He hadn't had any nightmares last night. Liam tensed at the implication of that tidbit of information. There could be a myriad of reasons that had come together to give him a blessedly peaceful night's sleep. Exhaustion. Great sex. Emotional upheaval. All three? *Or it could be Steele.* True.

The way Steele had taken over and cared for him baffled Liam's severely limited expectations. For as long as he could remember, nobody had ever cared enough about him to make the effort.

"That's a pretty intense expression after such a good night's sleep."

Liam jerked his head toward Steele. "Thinking about things."

"Yeah? What kind of things?" Steele stretched and pulled Liam up onto his shoulder. The bigger man ran his free hand over his stubbled chin and yawned.

"Good God, where do I start?"

"Start with what is putting that look on your face." Steele wound his foot through Liam's leg and pulled him closer. Liam melted into his cocoon of strong arms and tangled legs.

"When I was young."

"Childhood memories that bad?"

"Yeah, well, my father is the reverend of a small-town church in rural Georgia. My mom died while giving birth to my little brother, Aiden. I was four. Before my fifth birthday, my dad remarried. The woman, Vivian, hated me. I never understood why." Liam closed his eyes, recalling the images of his youth. "My father... I've always been a disappointment to him. He's hated who I am or what I remind him of for as long as I can remember. The beatings I got because he had a bad day, because Aiden didn't come home when he was supposed to, because Vivian said I didn't do my chores...hell, just for breathing. Well, it proved he couldn't stand to look at me. Vivian told me once it was because I looked like my mom."

"What happened to Aiden? Is he still in Georgia?"

Liam nodded and sighed. "Yeah, an acquaintance who isn't afraid of my father's judgment told me my brother lives in Atlanta now. She said he's a cop. Works in Homicide."

"I take it you two aren't close?"

"No. When I left for college, the scene with my father... well, by that point he'd figured out I was gay. He damned me to hell and told me not to come back unless I renounced my perversion. I tried to reach out to Aiden when I was in college. I sent several letters home and attempted to call a couple times to talk to him, but he never responded."

"Does Aiden share your father's views?"

"I really couldn't tell you. I wasn't allowed to spend much time with him. They kept us separated. I think Vivian liked Aiden, kept him with her. I regret not trying harder, but at the time, I was trying to make it through the day without being beaten. I hoped he knew and understood. When I graduated college, I applied to the Bureau and was accepted. I graduated from the academy. Being number one in my class, I got my choice of locations. I picked D.C. After my probationary period, I worked a couple of high profile cases and made a name for myself by being able to predict some of the movements of the criminals I had been assigned to track. Caleb James approached my supervising agent when they hit a dead end in Miller's case. The rest, as they say, is history."

"I think you're selling yourself short. I read your folder. The commendations you racked up in a short time prove that." The feel of Steele's lips on his hair sent a warm pulse through him.

"What about you?" Liam tipped his neck back in an attempt to see Steele's face.

"What about me?"

Liam pushed up on his elbow and pulled his hair out of his face. "Tell me something about you. You know way too much about me already. Give me something."

Steele reached up, tucked a wayward strand of hair back, and smiled. "I guess our information flow has been a little one-sided, hasn't it? What do you want to know?"

Liam dropped back down and tucked into Steele's shoulder. "Give me the SparkNotes version of Agent Steele McKenzie."

"SparkNotes, huh? Well, I have three sisters and a brother. All younger. My folks are typical middle-class parents. Dad is an electrical contractor. Mom teaches English at the high school we all attended. I played all the required sports in high school and college. Went into the Air Force after college. Did my time in an intelligence AFSC."

"AFSC?" Liam broke in, confused by the acronym.

"Air Force Specialty Code. Basically, a career field categorized by a set of numbers and letters. Which is basically just a way to say I worked in the intelligence field. The schools and contacts I made in the Air Force opened doors to my job at the Bureau."

"Do your parents know you're gay?"

"Yeah. Mom cried and hugged me almost to death the night I told them. She didn't want the homophobic assholes of the world to hurt me. Dad took it in stride. He nodded his head and patted me on the shoulder. As he walked out of the room he said, "'Hope you don't think that will get you out of giving your mom grandkids.'"

"I... I didn't think people like that existed." Liam's chest hurt. The admiration he felt for Steele's family filled him.

"Yeah, they're good people. My sisters are amazing and reproduce like rabbits. I have..." Steele lifted his eyes to the ceiling in thought. "Ten nieces and nephews. My brother is a bachelor and works on Wall Street doing some insanely boring job behind a desk. He's pulling in money hand over fist, but if you ask me, he's miserable."

"The majority of our work happens behind a desk."

"True, a cop's life is ninety-nine percent boredom. Honestly, it's not the one percent of pure 'Oh, fuck' that keeps me going either. I like the challenge of putting the puzzle together, working the evidence, tracking the clues, implications, suspicions. It's the mental portion that keeps me engaged."

Liam's hand played with the springy chest hairs under his fingers as he spoke. "I used to be like that too. I relished the chase. It's a pure rush when you figure out how or where. The why's didn't seem to show up very often."

"You ever think you'd come back to work at the Bureau?"

"No. Until a short time ago, I didn't think I'd leave my house for more than a couple hours. The thought of working again never crossed my mind."

"And now?"

"Now…"

Both men jumped at the sharp rap of knuckles on the bedroom door. Steele grabbed the sheet and pulled it up over both of them.

Masterson opened the door and gave them both a wide, cheesy smile. "Chief, Cole has called twice in the last hour. Told him you were indisposed. He told me to get you un-indisposed. This is me doing that."

"All right. I'll grab a shower and be down shortly."

Masterson smiled and winked. "I may be mistaken, because it's been a while, but if I recall correctly, shower sex is pretty awesome. Maybe I'll tell Cole you're doing some in-depth research?"

"Get the hell out of here."

Liam watched the pillow launch and hit the door Masterson was standing behind.

Masterson looked at the pillow and chuckled. "Hey, I'm only suggesting! Crap, is he always this grumpy in the morning? I don't think I'd put up with it. Maybe he needs coffee—with a ton of sugar—to sweeten his ass up."

Liam laughed when Steele lunged toward the door. Masterson slammed it before Steele even got out of the bed.

"Damn impertinent brat." Steele grumbled as he stood and stretched.

Liam let his eyes wander up and down the man's completely naked, chiseled body. He hadn't had a chance just to take in the entire man before, and he was definitely not letting the opportunity escape now. Steele had a chest and arms thick with muscle and dusted with dark brown, almost black, hair, abdominals any man would have to work years to develop, and an Adonis belt that drew his eye down to that meaty, delicious, long, thick cock. Liam saw it stir, plumping further under his lusty observation.

"Like what you see?"

"I do." Liam lay back on his elbows and glanced toward the bathroom.

"I've never had shower sex. Is it as good as Masterson recalls?" Liam's eyes drifted down, watching Steele's cock slowly become rigid. In the bright morning light, the man's girth reminded him why he ached this morning, and how he'd like to ache like that again.

"It's actually been years since I've had sex in the shower. Maybe, for the sake of current information, we should find out if Masterson is correct?"

"It is the only responsible thing to do."

"I concur."

"What about Cole?"

"Who?"

"The man who has called twice in the last hour?"

"Again I ask, who?" Steele extended his arm. Liam grabbed his hand and Steele pulled him out of the bed into the haven of Steele's warm body.

"You may piss off the powers that be."

"I know."

"You're going to get in trouble."

"Don't care."

"Why?

"Because some things are more important than the job."

"I'm not."

"You are."

"Why would you think that?" The idea that he was important enough for anyone to risk getting written up was entirely alien to Liam.

Steele brushed his hair away from his face. "How could you not?" The honest emotion in the man's eyes when he responded made Liam's breath catch.

Liam didn't know how to process what he saw. Instead, he stepped away from Steele and looked toward the bathroom.

"I don't know how to answer that."

Steele swooped in front of him and grabbed the his last remaining packet of lube from his wallet. He smiled and escorted Liam to the bathroom. The man's warm hand formed to the small of Liam's back. The mere touch sent a shiver up Liam's spine.

"You're cold. Let me turn on the shower and warm you up." Steele leaned into the massive shower and set the taps.

Liam couldn't suppress the smile that tugged at his lips. "I'm not cold. You did that."

"I did?" Steele turned and pulled Liam against him, their hard cocks brushing together. Liam closed his eyes and tilted his head. Steele found the junction of his throat and shoulder with his lips. Another shudder of anticipation trickled through him.

"Yes, you did." Liam slipped his arms around Steele's waist, then groaned. Steele thrust his thick, hard cock into Liam's, sending ripples of sensation through his body.

"I like that. I want to have good things happen to you." Steele's mouth traveled from Liam's neck to his lips. "I love it when you smile. I like thinking I had something to do with that."

Liam's tongue danced with Steele's, following as he was pulled into the shower. "Not something... everything."

"Can't take all the credit, baby. You've pulled yourself out of the hell you were in."

Baby, angel, whatever the endearment, Liam liked the pet names Steele had been calling him. He'd never had that before. Steele wrapped his hand around Liam's cock as he lowered his head to feast on Liam's whisker-sensitized shoulders.

Liam's brain short-circuited. Steele's hand on his cock and his lips on his body prevented any coherent conversation. "Want you." It was the best he could manage.

"You've got me, babe. I want you to face the wall, just like last night."

Liam nodded. He'd move as soon as Steele released his grip... maybe.

Steele chuffed a small burst of air and stepped away, allowing Liam to move. Thank God for the wall. At least it was solid. Liam placed his palms at shoulder level and leaned his cheek against the cool stone.

Steele separated his cheeks and licked at Liam's rim. Liam popped his head back from the tile. Steele, with his warm, hot tongue and those sexy-as-hell lips, licked, sucked, kissed and teased Liam's sensitive flesh... It was heaven and it was hell. He wanted more and he needed Steele to stop or he'd come.

Steele forced his tongue into Liam. "Oh fuck!" Liam slapped the wall with both hands and pushed his ass out, needing more. He reached for his cock, but Steele slapped his hand away.

"Mine." The man's growl preceded Steele's finger joining his tongue. Liam whimpered. The incredible sensations in him rolled and gained momentum. Steele added a second finger, never ceasing with the ravenous licking.

"Stop... going to come." He ground the warning out between his clenched teeth.

Steele doubled his efforts and twisted his fingers, reaching for and pushing against Liam's prostate. That was all it took. Liam clenched those fingers tight with his ass as his cock erupted. Cum sprayed against the wall and white spots exploded behind his eyelids.

Coming out of the orgasm-induced bliss, Liam realized Steele had lifted off his knees and now had Liam's limp body trapped against his chest. The man's impressive hard-on was trapped between Liam's cheeks.

"If you're too sore from last night, I can finish just like this." Steele rocked his hips, forcing his cock through the crevice of Liam's ass.

"No. Want you."

Liam heard the tell-tale crinkle of the lube packet. Steele's lips assaulted his neck and jaw, peppering kisses between nips and scrapes of that glorious prickly stubble. Steele belted his arms around Liam and held him tightly at the same time his hot cock pressed at his entrance. The initial push burned. Steele was so damn thick that the intrusion brought more than a little pain. Liam gasped and Steele froze.

"Tell me when, baby. When you're ready." Steele's voice had lowered at least two octaves. Liam swallowed hard and concentrated on breathing, waiting for his muscles to relax. He nodded and Steele pushed forward while he bore down. The intense burn became a precarious pain that bordered on the promise of bliss. Fully seated, Steele once again stilled, but Liam needed him to move.

"Fuck me, Steele. Fuck me hard. I want to feel you all day."

"Are you sure?" Steele retreated slowly, his cock on a slow sensuous slide as he asked.

"Yeah, need it hard." Liam felt Steele's hand on his back, pushing him forward. Liam braced against the wall and Steele slammed into Liam's body, lancing him with his rigid cock. The man's wide girth brushed Liam's prostate with damn near every forward lunge. There was no gentleness, no waiting or reassurances. Steele pounded into Liam—fucking him hard, feral in his own need. The smell of sex and the hard-driven grunts of both men permeated the tile-lined room.

Steele's thrusting became erratic. He curled his body over Liam's. There was no way the hands at Liam's hips weren't going to leave bruises. Steele pulled Liam back hard as he slammed forward. He raged out an animalistic growl when Liam's body clenched tightly as he came again. The man hammered into Liam, riding him through his orgasm. Steele jacked up hard into Liam and ground out a low groan as he came. Liam couldn't feel Steele's cum inside him, but knowing it was there and that Miller never would be again set him free on so many levels.

Stilling, Steele pulled Liam into him and rested his forehead on Liam's shoulder. "Holy hell, that was fucking amazing."

Steele's cock softened and slipped free. Liam dropped his head back and blinked up at the ceiling. "I think you need to thank Masterson for the suggestion."

"Like hell I will. That man gets no credit for this."

"Maybe I'll thank him, then." Liam gasped when Steele spun him around.

"Nope. You can thank me. Later, tonight. Hopefully several times tonight."

"I could be enticed."

"It takes enticement?"

"Yep." Liam leaned forward and kissed Steele. The man chased Liam's lips. When Liam laughed at his failed attempt to capture them, Steele wrapped his hands in Liam's wet hair and forced his mouth open with his tongue—hot, demanding and entirely male. Steele pulled away only when breathing became an issue.

"Enticement enough?"

"For now." His panted response was as close to a challenge as he could get. Liam watched Steele lift that one eyebrow again. God, the subtle move was pure sex.

"Really?"

"Yeah, I'm thinking that type of enticement at regular intervals throughout the day may be required." Liam peeked up at the man through his lashes.

"Oh, Mr. Mercier, I do like the way you think."

CHAPTER 10

*S*teele's good mood shattered as soon as he hit the stairs. His supervisor's voice drifted up to where he stood. Agent Cole Davis had been assigned as his supervisor for about three months. During that time, they'd met a couple of times, but Steele's caseload and Cole's new supervisory duties had had them running in different directions. The talks they'd had were cordial, and Steele had gotten the feeling that the agent waiting for him was damn good at his job. Without a doubt, sending his supervisor here was the brass's move to force Steele to use Liam as bait. Steele closed his eyes and cracked his neck, readying himself for the fight he knew was inevitable.

He drew a deep breath and entered the library. Steele caught a smirk on Masterson's face before his agent made a hasty exit, following the rest of his team. Smart man. It took Steele a moment before he acknowledged his supervisor, and that was because he didn't recognize him. Cole, a branch chief who was on course to become a deputy director, wore jeans, a T-shirt, ball cap and tennis shoes. He looked a solid ten years younger than he had when they'd met in Cole's office. Standing beside him was a younger man who had the physical markers of someone with Down syndrome.

"Steele, good to see you again. This is my brother-in-law Frankie. Frankie, say hello to Agent McKenzie."

A broad smile spread across the young man's face. "Hello, Agent. Do you work with Cole?"

"I sure do. He's my boss." Steele took Frankie's hand and stage whispered, "But I like him anyway."

Frankie laughed. "I like him too."

Cole put a hand on Frankie's shoulder. "Hey, bud, could you wait for me over there by the windows? I need to talk to Steele for a minute about police business."

"Police business is important. I'll wait." The young man walked to the window, put his hands in his pockets and watched the landscaping crew that was currently trimming the manicured bushes of the estate.

"Sorry for inserting myself into your investigation, Steele, but the brass is breathing down my neck. Hell, they called me on vacation just to chew my ass. For some reason, the old men are hell bent on putting Mercier on the street to lure Miller out in the open. Care to tell me why?"

Steele glanced up as Liam walked into the room. He waited for Liam to make his way over to them.

"This is Liam Mercier. Liam, my supervisor, Cole Davis." Steele watched as Liam threw up his defenses. He stepped back and looked down as he nodded, not extending his hand in greeting.

"Agent Mercier, I'm honored to meet you. Thank you for what you've given to the Bureau. I understand there have been lasting ramifications." Cole's comment didn't carry an ounce of condemnation.

"I'm not an agent any longer." Liam's calm reply didn't throw Steele's supervisor.

"I realize that. Thank you for assisting us."

Liam shrugged. "Not like I had a choice."

Cole whipped his head toward Steele. "Explain that."

"Orders." Steele caught a glimpse of Phil making his way toward Frankie and jerked his head toward the brewing situation. "Liam, your attack cat." Liam's eyes widened and he headed toward the cat to stave off whatever the little rat bastard had planned.

"What the fuck did he mean that he didn't have a choice?" The hissed question sounded under Cole's breath.

Steele turned and lowered his voice too. "Caruthers directed me to tell him his benefits would be stopped if he didn't cooperate and assist us with this case. The man was hunkered down in a house that could double as a nuclear bunker, and I don't know if the second coming of Christ could have leveraged him out of that fortress. But that bastard threatened his income and he had to leave the only security he's had for the last five years. He's making it work, but damn it, I've fucked up several times. Triggers I didn't know he had blew up on us. The man's fucking strong, though. He's adapting."

"Son of a bitch." Cole pulled his phone out and started messing with the screen.

"Yeah." Steele agreed with the curse.

"This is Agent Cole Davis, I need to speak to Director Hayes." Steele did a double take. One *did not* just call the freaking director of the FBI. It just didn't happen.

"When? All right. No, it's urgent, but it can wait until then. Thank you." Cole ended the call and pocketed the phone.

"Hayes will call me back when he gets back from his weekly POTUS brief. In the meantime, bring me up to speed on the case. Where are you, what have you done, what's the next step and how can I help?"

Steele shook his head and chuckled. Running a hand

through his hair, he cast a glance at his supervisor. "You're not what I expected, and I thank God for that. Right now, we are up to our elbows in raw data and the tip line is pulling two to three hundred calls a day. I have some newbs just out of the academy filtering those." Steele walked over to the long table and whiteboards where his team had started sorting through the mass of information.

"Man, if only this shit was as easy as it is portrayed on television. Okay, I get the info sifting. Assuming the tips don't pan out, what's the next step?"

"Next step? As far as the team goes, we are searching for some of the same criteria Liam used to pinpoint Miller the first time. Right now, I'm focusing on working that information to find any indication of Miller. With the background Liam was able to give us, we have an idea where to start. We are looking for an abandoned location with power. Miller will need medical supplies. We're covering hospitals, medical equipment warehouses, suppliers, etc. Plus, we are monitoring every law enforcement channel and watching reports of missing people who match his MO."

Cole glanced over his shoulder at Liam and Frankie. "What is Miller really after? Another kill or him?"

"He left a note when he escaped. He wants Liam. I don't agree with the brass's methods, but they have a point. It's only a matter of time before Miller makes a play to find him or draw him out. We are going to try to turn that situation. If we can get a hit on a possible location or general area, we have a chance in narrowing our options. Until then, our position is secure—or it was. How did you find us?"

"Masterson. The third time I called, he gave it up. I didn't write it down, nor did I call in my location. You're still off the grid. Damn fine safe house, though. How'd you get it?"

"Masterson knows the owner."

"Huh, friends in high places."

"Or friends who are rock star royalty. This is Lucifer Cross's estate."

"No shit?"

"Yeah. I'm not going to put Liam in danger again. He's already given too much."

"True. He's paid his dues, many times over. The pressure you had to pull him from his safety is concerning. Frankly, it stinks of someone—or maybe several people—covering their asses."

"Speaking of that, you might want to talk with Dr. Morgan and Caleb James. They know a hell of a lot more about the events that led up to his capture by Miller. I have a feeling someone made a political play by ousting an unwanted competitor using Liam as a pawn."

Cole closed his eyes and squeezed the bridge of his nose between his fingers. "Hell, man, the political maneuvering is rampant." He dropped his hand and pierced Steele with his gaze. "I'll send that information up the right channels and make sure it's looked into. I know the new director and he doesn't do business like the good ole boys who are pressuring you." Cole rubbed the back of his neck and took a deep breath before he continued. "So this is what's going to happen. I'm going to have a heart-to-heart with the director and you are going to locate and capture an escaped serial killer. I've got your back. Get the job done. I'll leave the methodology to you. I'll give you a word of advice, though."

The weight of the world lifted off Steele's shoulders. He was actually at a loss for words. His supervisor had single-handedly reinstated his faith in the Bureau. He'd gladly accept the man's advice. "What's that?"

"Don't marginalize Mercier." Cole lifted his hand, stopping the automatic denial Steele wanted to throw at him. "I know he's been through enough shit to last a couple lifetimes, but if you define him by *your* belief of what *he* is capable of, you're only hurting him and this investigation. I know he's not ours anymore, but for this case, treat him like a full-fledged agent. Allow him not only to advise, but also to participate. I have a feeling he may be the key to a successful resolution." Cole's direct stare spoke volumes. Steele felt a river of apprehension run up his spine at what his supervisor was asking.

"What if he can't handle the pressure?"

"Let *him* tell you that, McKenzie. He's brilliant—hesitant and abused, but brilliant. Allow him to be that man again. Sometimes it's faith and support we need, not coddling and protection."

"Thank you." Steele needed to say that.

"For what?"

"Allowing me to do my job—the right way. And giving a shit about him. Not many have."

"I've had experience in dealing with people who have been traumatized like Mercier. Besides, this is what they put me in this position to do. The director is a straight shooter with no skeletons hanging in his closet. The political machine doesn't have anything on him to make him sway one way or the other. He's newly appointed, so change will be slow, but things will be different. The old guard is in for a ride. They're either going to come around or they'll be gone. We have the people in place now to effect a real change and get us back to the law enforcement organization that we used to be. I have faith. You should too." Cole slapped Steele on the shoulder. "As far as Mercier is concerned, he's one of us. Period. We have to take care of our own. You and I aren't the same as the suits in the corner offices, and they are struggling to hold onto the reins of a horse that is changing directions. Keep the faith, McKenzie. Better days are coming."

"Seems like it's been a hell of a long time since I had any hope, let alone faith. But you keep the brass off me and we'll get this bastard." Steele glanced toward Liam and gave a huff of laughter at the scene. Liam and Frankie sat on the floor with Phil lolling over Frankie's lap. The damn stealth ninja feline assassin was playing with a string like a kitten. "I guess I'm the only one that fleabag hates."

"Sounds like a personal problem, Steele. I'm out of here."

~

LIAM HAD REACHED Phil just as the cat leaned against the leg of the young man standing by the window. He pulled Phil up into his arms. The cat started his ground-shaking purr immediately. Liam knuckled Phil's head and the cat nearly turned himself inside out writhing in joy.

"She's a big kitty."

Liam glanced at the young man. "This is Phil. A boy cat. He's very big and a bit of a bully sometimes."

"A bully?"

"Yeah, see that guy over there?"

"I met him. Cole introduced us. My name's Frankie."

"Hi, Frankie, I'm Liam."

"Nice to meet you, Liam. Why is your kitty a bully? He purrs loud."

"He does. Phil sometimes wants his own way, and he's not very nice if he doesn't get what he wants." Liam glanced over at Steele and his supervisor, wondering whether or not he should be wishing he could be part of the conversation. His mind refused to go there. After all, he wasn't an agent, just a person with information. Hell, that really wasn't fair. He'd been treated well after he'd been removed from his house. Steele had been... amazing.

"Why are you sad?"

Frankie reached out and pet Phil's belly. Surprisingly, His

Royal Highness seemed to approve of the attention and ratcheted up the volume of his motorboat purr.

"Why do you think I'm sad?" Damn, he'd put up a good front. Hadn't he?

"Logan used to be very sad too. She was lonely. Cole made her happy."

"Who's Logan?" Liam was trying to keep up, but the kid had lost him.

"My sister. She was a cop. She was always sad, like you. She got married. Cole makes her happy. Maybe you should be someone's husband. That way you'll be happy."

"I don't think it works that way, Frankie." Liam wished it did.

"Yes, it does. Logan says life is too short to be sad. Find what makes you happy, Frankie. Hold onto it tight, she says. Who makes you happy? You should tell them and hold on tight and then you won't be sad anymore." Frankie lifted Phil out of his arms and sat down on the floor with the cat in his lap.

Liam sank to the ground and glanced at Steele. Simplistic, but the kid had a point.

"I like your marks."

Liam glanced at Frankie. The young man pointed to the heart and ivy scars on his arm.

"They're pretty. I like them. Why do you cover them up?" Liam pulled at his sleeve, tugging the shirt down farther. A string pulled free from the frayed hoodie. He gave it to Frankie to tease Phil. "I don't like them. They remind me of someone bad."

"Logan says bad people just happen. Sometimes they hurt you and sometimes they hurt other people. She says when they hurt you, at least they aren't hurting someone else. Sometimes we need to be strong so other people aren't hurt. That's what Logan says."

Liam stared at the man sitting with him on the floor—innocence incarnate. Logan must be a sage and a wonderful woman if this young man was any indication.

"It sounds like Logan is a very smart woman." Liam's voice was thick with emotion.

"Yeah. Cole says she's too smart sometimes, but we don't tell her that."

Liam laughed. Yeah, he just bet that didn't get shared. He'd wager anything Frankie wouldn't keep a thing from his sister.

"Ready to go, Frankie?" Cole's called from the other side of the room.

"Yes." He lifted Phil off his lap and kissed the cat's head. "Goodbye, Phil. Don't be a bully." He set the cat down and they both stood before Frankie wrapped his arms around Liam. "Goodbye. Don't be sad."

Liam hugged the young man back. "Goodbye, Frankie. I'll try my best."

"Good. Logan says you can only do your best."

"Logan's right."

Frankie smiled hugely and waved as he walked across the room. Liam nodded toward Cole as the man took Frankie's hand and strolled out the door.

"He seemed to like you." Steele cast a wary eye toward Phil, who had jumped up onto the windowsill.

"Sweet kid."

"Cole is flying top cover, but we need to kick this manhunt into high gear. I know you've given us the information we need to do this search, but I'd like to put you to work on the team. I need your experience and your gut feelings on this one. Do you think you'd be able to do it without..."

"Without freaking out? Turning into a blithering idiot?" Liam hated the idea that Steele and his team had witnessed his meltdowns. Anger pooled in his gut. Feeling emasculated morphed his humiliation into something more visceral. He was letting what Miller had done to him keep him from being who he was, who he could be. Yet he didn't know how to get back to what he had been.

"Hey, where did you go?" Steele stepped closer and placed his hands on Liam's hips, crooking his head to meet Liam's gaze.

"I hate what I am. What he made me." Liam broke the eye contact. Steele didn't need to see the utter worthlessness he felt.

"Then let's not let *him* define *you*. I want and need you on my team. We'll work within your limitations. You are the key to getting this bastard." Steele pulled Liam closer by tugging his jeans' belt loops. "But you need to understand something. This thing we have… It's not dependent on you working with us. I want this—what's between us. Period. Help or don't. I'm not giving up on us."

Steele's lips found that spot behind Liam's ear that sent a shiver down his spine.

"Me or the cold?" The question was whispered, a mere breath between them.

"You. Definitely you."

"Ahh…excuse me, boss, but can we get back to work?" Masterson's voice from the doorway earned a groan from Liam and a laugh from Steele.

"Yeah, get your asses back in here. We have work to do." Steele let go of Liam but whispered, "The enticement you required is going to have to wait. We have a job to do."

Liam took a deep breath, did a gut check and headed toward where the team was gathering. If only life *could* be as simple as Frankie thought it was.

CHAPTER 11

Steele stood and stretched. Seven hours stooping over information and data points had fried his brain and nuked his back. He lifted his arms over his head and clasped his fingers together, stretching as far up as he could reach. Leaning to the left, he allowed his eyes to seek out Liam. Steele's mind raced with bits and pieces of information, but the sight of the man slogging through the same spreadsheets and mountains of information just like his team gave him a sense of immense pride and contentment.

Sunday was the staff's night off, so he'd sent Masterson, Fleming and Hardin to get take-out. Actually, he'd sent Fleming as the low man on the totem pole. Hardin and Masterson had decided they needed a break and gone with her. They'd left so quickly he had to give Liam the Masterson's cell phone number so he could call to make sure their orders were right. Steele couldn't blame them for getting the hell away from the mountains of information. It was suffocating at times.

The tedious work of an investigator wasn't the fast-paced glitz and glamor and 'aha!' moments portrayed by beautiful actors who solved heinous crimes in sixty minutes or less. No, being an investigator—a good one—was more like putting together a puzzle that was comprised of one solid color. You worked the pieces until you knew them intimately and then looked for a way they flowed together flawlessly. Unfortunately, sometimes they never did. What a real investigator did was in no way easy and rarely dramatic. It took a determined effort to link even one or two pieces of the crime together. Right now, they had the border of their puzzle worked. The frame of the crime and the criminal they knew. It was the middle of the picture that was eluding Steele. Somehow, he wasn't seeing the forest for the trees. He needed to step back and regroup—get back to the basics.

Steele walked over to the largest whiteboard in the room. He clicked a picture of it with his phone and started erasing the scribbled notes his team had made throughout the day. He needed to fall back to Intelligence Gathering 101. He labeled the board—Basic Facts, Evidence, Methodology—Miller's, Locations and Victimology—Miller's.

Liam tossed his pencil onto the stack of paper he was currently wading through. Liam's tired gaze drifted toward him, then rested on the board. "Good idea. I'm inundated with minutia and my cognitive reasoning is suspect at best right now."

Steele wrapped his hand around the back of his neck and rubbed. "Recapping like this before we call it a night might give us some momentum going into tomorrow."

Steele extended a hand and crooked his finger at Liam. The man's face took on a flush of pink, but he rose and walked over.

"I think we need a break too," Steele said as he pulled Liam into him and buried his nose in the hair lying on Liam's neck. He didn't even try to hide the long, deep breath he pulled into his lungs. Damn, the man smelled of warm body and sensuous musk, and he still had the subtle smell of the body wash they'd used that morning after Steele had staked his claim on his lover in the shower. He could get used to this, and if he had his way, he would. Now all he needed to do was capture a killer. Oh, and convince the man in his arms he should give them both a chance at a future... together.

Liam pulled away slightly to chase Steele's lips. Steele was onboard with that idea. The kiss, soft and lazy, given and received as comfort and validation, lasted an eternity. Steele's hands softly caressed Liam, exploring, touching and learning. The front door alarm chirped and his team's laughter tumbled through the hallway.

Liam sighed and tried to pull away. Steele didn't release him. Instead, he pulled the man closer and gave him a final kiss. "Later." His whispered promise left his lips as he released Liam and turned toward the whiteboard.

Masterson and Fleming carried bags of Chinese take-out while Hardin followed them in with two six packs of beer.

"Good thing I answered your phone call, Liam. I almost didn't because I didn't recognize the number. Dipshit over there didn't hear you ask for beef and broccoli." Masterson grabbed an eggroll and shoved half of it into his mouth.

"Fuck you, man. You didn't hear him either." Hardin tossed Liam and Steele each a beer.

"Hey, that's an awesome fucking idea, chief. I need to see the data points on the board. It's like I can't focus on the snowflake because of the massive drift I've been walking through." Masterson opened the containers and passed out the plates, chopsticks and silverware. He eyed the board and munched on what remained of his egg roll.

"Yeah, hey, pass my shrimp fried rice." Steele filled his plate and sat next to Liam. At least Liam's appetite seemed to be returning. His plate held an eggroll and some beef and broccoli. Steele actually wondered how the man maintained such a ripped body with so little food. Maybe it was the meds after all. Since Liam had stopped taking them, he'd eaten more.

Steele popped a crab rangoon into his mouth and spoke around the hot filling. "I want to put it all up on the board after dinner."

Hardin popped some lo mien into his mouth and talked around the noodles. "Okay, but Angela gets to transcribe. By the way, your handwriting sucks, chief."

Steele shrugged, but Fleming sent a chopstick flying at Hardin. "So fucking stereotypical of you, ass wipe. Just 'cause I'm a girl you assume I'm going to dot my 'i's' with little hearts too?"

Masterson ducked as the wooden chopstick flew back toward Fleming. "No, sweet Jesus, you're touchy today. You're doing it because you're the jeepest. Shit, woman, it rolls downhill."

"Oh, well, okay then." Fleming's Jersey accented voice mollified somewhat.

Liam leaned back in his chair and put his feet on the table. He glanced at Steele and nodded toward Hardin. "Jeepest?"

"Newest troop. If you're new, you're jeep. Have no idea where the term comes from, but it is pretty common among all the military branches."

"Well, to be fair then, that makes me the transcriber." Liam shoved the last of his eggroll into his mouth and stood. He moved toward the board and picked up a dry erase pen. Chewing his food, he looked at the first column. Steele couldn't help the smirk on his face. Hell yeah, Liam taking initiative. He liked watching as the man Liam used to be came out of that shell he'd been shoved into.

The basic facts and evidence column filled quickly. All

were indisputable, but starting with the known and extrapo-lating couldn't hurt. The next column was Miller's Method-ology. Liam had covered that in his briefing. To his credit, Liam did a bullet point listing under the topic header. Liam turned toward the Locations column.

Steele halted the team's inputs. "Wait. Let's look at the methodology again for a minute. If we discount the things Miller did, what is the reason he did them? What did the shrinks say? Why the need for the scroll work? Do we have anything on what caused him to break away from his former life? Does he have family that can tell us about him before he turned into the sick fuck he is?"

Hardin started pulling folders from the bottom of a two-foot-high stack. "I got some of that, chief. He was a prodigy. Got a full ride to med school. Up and leaves school during his fourth year and his family reports him missing. His mother, now deceased, called the cops when he showed up just over a year later. He never accounted for the time he was gone, at least not to the authorities. He shows back up. Goes back to school, but switches his degree and becomes a nurse anesthetist."

Liam lifted his hand, pointing to Hardin. "That's right. I was going to work that angle, but I got a hit on the ware-house. I wanted to see if there were any unsolved murders of gay men during the year he was missing. But you'd probably need to confine the search to missing men during that period matching my description. That's one thing he's never wavered on."

Masterson hit the computer and called up the database. "Where did he disappear from? Where's home? Where did he go to school?"

"Akron, Ohio," Liam said, just as Harding spoke. "He attended college in Ohio."

Angela squeaked with her bottle of beer halfway to her

lips. "Did he have a boyfriend in medical school? If he did…
what did he look like, and is he still alive?"

Steele watched his team feed off each other. Liam fit into
the interaction seamlessly.

Steele nodded toward Angela before he spoke. "Running
with a hunch here, but if Miller fixated on someone and that
person left—say… graduated or flunked out—based on his
personality disorders, he'd go after him… track him down,
stalk him. How far back can we track restraining orders?
Miller wasn't using an alias in medical school. Get one of the
computer experts on the cybercrimes side to work every
restraining order in a three-state radius of Ohio during the
period Miller was missing. If we get a hit, that's where we'll
start the search for the boyfriend."

Steele's team scurried, writing or tapping on tablets and
computers. Liam, however, stood with his hands on his hips
and stared at the ground. He shook his head and turned back
toward the board.

"Liam, what's running through your mind?" Steele's question set every eye toward the whiteboard.

Liam shrugged and took a deep breath, puffing his cheeks
out as he exhaled. He cast a glance at Steele.

"I was serious this morning. You are part of this team. I
need your intuition, your gut feelings, whatever it is that is
causing you to pause. Spit it out."

"All right. Well, the background on Miller's past is good
for information and may help us understand his motivation,
but I can't help feeling that what started him isn't what is
driving him now."

"Okay, let's go with that. What *is* driving him now?" The
room fell silent, every eye on Liam.

Liam glanced around and lowered his eyes. "I am."

"We know that you're unfinished business, but he's
escaped, free and on the run. Everything in his psych profile

says he'll start the process again. He'll kill again. We know how he does it. We can get in front of him." Masterson's statement dropped into the now uncommonly quiet brainstorming session. It seemed like nobody wanted to scare Liam into not speaking.

"Yeah, about that. I don't think he is... on the run, I mean. What if I led you down the wrong path when I suggested we concentrate on how I found him? Are we wasting time and man-hours searching for an anomaly that isn't going to appear? Are we chasing our tails? After all, he knows how I found him. He won't make the same mistake."

"Then what do you suggest we do?" Steele leaned back in his chair, trying to appear relaxed, but he had a feeling he knew what Liam was going to suggest.

"Put me in front of some cameras. Let me talk to him directly."

Steele was on his feet in a heartbeat. "Oh, hell no. I'm not using you as bait. I fought that war and won. You've paid your dues."

Liam put his hands in the front pocket of his hoodie before he straightened his shoulders and looked directly at Steele. With a strength in his voice that Steele hadn't heard before, Liam spoke. "Yeah, well a very smart young man once told me that when bad people hurt you, at least they aren't hurting someone else. Sometimes we need to be strong so other people aren't hurt. I know I can't begin to live again, be free from my past, until Miller's no longer a threat. Besides, I don't know if I could live with myself if someone else was put through what he did to me because he couldn't get to me. I trust that you and your team will have my back. Regardless, I'm the best play we have if we want to end this without further lives being sacrificed. As much as I hate to agree with the bastards that threatened my existence to get me here... they *were* right."

Steele stood stunned. As if the curtain had been lifted away, he could see the man Liam used to be. "You're walking into the lion's den. Voluntarily. You realize that, don't you?"

Liam nodded. "Did I ever tell you my middle name?" Steele shook his head, amazed at the confidence he sensed in his lover. "It's Daniel. Now, how about we script this bitch and move from defense to offense?"

CHAPTER 12

Two sets of tired eyes looked at the whiteboard. They'd worked the plan through the night. He'd chased his team upstairs about three hours ago. Dead tired they would be useless today and he needed someone to be able to function. The sun rose, painting an orange and pink tinted haze over the room.

"I still don't like it." Steele snapped the objection toward Liam. He'd been fighting against this course of action every step of the way.

"You're being unreasonable." Liam's soft reply chided Steele, and he didn't like that either.

"Too many variables." The plan exposed Liam in ways he didn't need. All the other factors notwithstanding, the media could rake him over the coals. The questions could trigger another anxiety attack. He could just imagine Liam puking or passing out on national television. Fuck, this whole situation sucked.

"I'll never be alone. You'll have eyes or guns on me at all times. Hell, you'll be right beside me." If Liam's comment was supposed to reassure him, it failed epically. He'd seen Liam dissolve. Steele would never remind him of that fact.

"And how does that stop the sick fuck from doing something we didn't anticipate?" The anger and frustration he felt radiated around him. He didn't want to expose Liam, and that was clouding his ability to look at the plan on the board objectively. He knew it and Liam knew it, but at this point, he didn't give a shit.

Liam bumped his shoulder with his own. "Hey, it's a good plan. I trust you to do what you need to do to keep me safe. You have to trust me to keep my shit together long enough to do what I need to do."

Steele turned and pinned Liam with a stare. "It wasn't that long ago you lost it at the smell of a latex glove and passed the fuck out when you heard the powers that be wanted to set you up as bait. Now you just magically expect me to be okay with taking you out of a secure area and putting you in front of a mass of media barracudas? They won't pull any punches, Liam. This is not going to happen. I can't deal with your issues in an uncontrolled environment!"

Liam jerked away from his side as if he'd been slapped. "My issues are just that, *my* issues. Let *me* worry about them. You worry about catching Miller." His voice rose with each word until he shouted Miller's name.

Some part of Steele's mind registered that his actions were the exact opposite of what he needed to do, but he was too damn tired and upset to give more than a passing acknowledgement. Fuck caring why. "You aren't ready. I'm not going to allow it."

Liam marched past him and slapped away Steele's hand when he tried to stop him. "Where the hell do you think you're going?"

"I'm leaving."

"Like hell you are." Steele's grumbled warning came out low and dangerous.

Liam turned. His chest rose and fell with heavy breaths. "Really? Am I under arrest?"

"What? What the fuck are you talking about?"

"Am I in custody? Am I being held here?" Liam shouted the questions. His face flushed a heated hue of crimson.

"Held? No, you know better than that! What the fuck are you talking about?"

"I'm leaving." Liam spun on his heel and made it two steps before Steele bolted into action.

"Over my fucking dead body! That bastard is out there hunting you!" Steele's shouted reprimand didn't faze Liam. The smaller man wrenched his arm away from Steele's vise-like grip.

"Exactly! But instead of taking the hunt to him and giving us an advantage, you'd rather treat me like I'm going to break. Well, here's some news for you, Special Agent in Charge McKenzie. I just may break. But if I do, it will be doing something to stop this psychotic motherfucker. I'm sick and tired of being terrified." Liam raked both hands through his hair and fisted it in his anger. "Don't you fucking understand? Do you have any idea what it is like being trapped, more dead than alive? No, *you don't* and you *never* will! This is a good plan. I guess the shit you've been spouting about me being stronger than I give myself credit for was just a lie. I guess that makes me strong enough to fuck but not mentally competent enough to work as a part of your actual team. I got the message loud and clear. Get the hell out of my way and stay away from me!"

Liam shoved his way past as his angry words echoed into the sudden silence. Steele roared in frustration. The anguished sound did nothing to alleviate the tension binding him. Holy fuck, how did trying to protect Liam from being hurt again turn into this?

Steele was pounding up the stairs after Liam before he could even think to question whether or not it was a good idea. Liam's bedroom door slammed as he crested the stairs. Steele drew up to the door within seconds and turned the handle. Locked. He reared back and kicked the strike plate of the door. The oak slab hit the inside wall with a shattering groan.

Liam stood frozen and wide-eyed in the middle of the room. Steele strode across the room and grabbed the man by the back of his neck and bicep. "You've got it all wrong. I don't think you're weak. You are the strongest man I know. You're right that I don't understand what you've gone through. I only know I don't want you going through any more."

"That's not up to you." The words ground out through his clenched teeth. Liam's anger ran deep.

"I know, and I don't like it."

"What you like or don't like doesn't matter. *I* don't matter. Getting Miller has to be the *only* objective." Liam relaxed slightly in his grip.

"You *do* matter. To me. To me, you matter." Steele searched Liam's expression, hoping his words got through.

"And you matter to me. I have to do this. You know I do."

"Yeah. I just...yeah, I do." Steele dropped his forehead to Liam's. The defeat he didn't want to face had him in a choke-hold and that bastard tightened his grip. God, he wished there was another way.

"Set it up."

"I don't want to do this to you, Liam. I don't know what I'd do if you were hurt again." Steele couldn't bear the thought of anyone hurting his lover.

"This really isn't about you or me. It never has been. It's

about Miller—catching him before he can hurt anyone else. If we don't do this and someone else is hurt or killed, could you live with yourself?" Liam leaned into Steele and rested on his shoulder.

Steele wrapped his arms around him and drew Liam closer. "I can't lose you."

"Then do your job, Steele. I have faith in you." Liam pulled away and walked into the bathroom, shutting the door behind him. Steele was at the door in two steps. His hand gripped the doorknob. No, fuck... Liam was right. He didn't like it, didn't want it to happen, but damn it, he'd have to play the cards he held. Steele thumped his head against the closed door and drew a deep breath, then another. It took every fucking ounce of self-restraint he had, but he managed to release his grip from the door handle.

Steele turned on his heel and headed downstairs. Each step he took was toward a destiny he didn't want for Liam—but one he couldn't prevent.

CHAPTER 13

$\mathcal{L}$iam glanced out the small gap left by the partially opened door at the sea of faces. The microphone arrays being set up nearly obliterated his view of the reporters, but they were there. An elevated bank of news cameras stared at the platform where he would be standing after the local police chief took the stage. The blank lenses of the cameras were waiting to capture his words and send them directly to Miller. Liam shut the door and leaned his forehead onto the cool wood. The plan was solid. Keeping that in mind became paramount. His team wouldn't let him down—this time. Hardin and Fleming, along with three other agents, patrolled the room. He'd be safe. He knew what they were doing. Several levels of security checked and rechecked faces and credentials. There was no way Miller knew he was here, in this place at this time. He wouldn't be in the audience, and yet anxiety gripped Liam's chest and made breathing hard.

Steele hadn't left his side, and for that, he was thankful. He glanced over at his… lover? Team leader? Protector? Hell, any label Liam slapped on what they had… It wasn't quite right. Nothing fit. But that wasn't surprising. Since Agent McKenzie had showed up at his door, nothing made sense. How could one person fall for another so quickly? Love at first sight didn't happen. Lust at first sight? Well, *that* might happen, but he wasn't so sure he'd actually lusted after Steele at first sight. He actually didn't remember much until after he'd visited the crime scene, where he'd puked his guts out. Yeah, Liam had absolutely no clue why Steele was attracted to him. Lord knew the man had seen him at his worst.

"Hey, you okay? You're looking through me." Steele's voice broke through his musings.

"What? Oh, yeah, yeah, I'm fine. I was just thinking about things. Been one hell of a ride." Liam looked out from his hidden position again to the crowd of reporters who were enthralled with the statement the police chief was making.

"Where's Masterson?" Liam hadn't seen the agent since early that morning.

"One of the newbs got a hit from one of the local police departments on some stolen medical equipment. Someone took a semi from a truck stop but abandoned it about fifty miles up the interstate. The driver and cops didn't notice anything out of place so the driver did the report and took the load to the delivery point. When they off loaded the equipment, they noticed some of the items we had high-lighted as potential targets were missing."

"Some?" Liam's skin crawled and his gut clenched.

"According to the report, all but a few items taken were on the list of things he would need to continue. Sam headed out to interview the driver and the local cops. He's supposed to keep us updated."

Liam nodded. "He's late checking in?"

Steele glanced at his watch and shrugged. Liam sensed

Steele wasn't telling him the entire truth. Why? Probably overprotective. *Liam, let it go. For now.* "Well, at least we know Miller will see the interview."

Steele cleared his throat. "Just the statement, Liam. You're following the official briefing. The media is buzzing. You'll be fresh meat to them. They didn't get to drag you through the mire during the last trial. You won't take questions."

"I know. But Miller needs to see me. If he does, he may not fixate on a surrogate. If we can keep him coming after me, we can mitigate collateral damage. After this conference, I'll make some public outings like we planned. Get him to come after me."

"Maybe. There is no guarantee Miller won't change his methodology or victimology."

Steele's reasoning was faulty. Liam knew it, so did Steele. "His rituals are everything to him. Even if his motivation for the killings has changed and I'm his focus, the rituals are still his world. If we focus on what's important to him, like his rituals, play to his needs and his habits and obsessions, we'll find him."

Liam jumped when the Bureau's PR rep stepped into the protected area where he and Steele waited.

"Okay, it's time." The woman spoke to them, but her eyes were glued to the tablet she carried. "The major players are all here and the police chief will be wrapping up his questions soon. He's only out there to make an appearance. The reporters have been briefed you will only be giving a statement. I know they will definitely disregard my instructions and throw questions at you as soon as you finish. Just walk off the stage. Stick to your script. Impromptu performances rarely go well when the piranhas are circling."

Liam nodded and took a deep breath. Steele thanked the woman and asked for a moment alone. Steele spun Liam and held him tight. Before he had a chance to lean into the hug, Steele's lips captured his in a forceful kiss. Abruptly Steele released him and he gulped for air.

"What was that about?"

"You're mine, not his. I just wanted that on your mind when you read that statement." Steele opened the door for Liam and winked. Liam blinked at the agent and shook his head. He took as deep a breath as he could and walked to the lectern.

Liam took in the reporters with an encompassing sweep before he lifted the paper in his hands.

"My name is Liam Mercier. Five years ago, I was an agent with the Federal Bureau of Investigation. My team, at that time, apprehended Stuart Miller. Due to particular events I will not go into, I was Miller's last victim. He held me for thirteen days."

Liam paused for several seconds before he pulled his sweatshirt off. The tight white T-shirt he wore underneath it allowed the cameras to capture the red and silver scar tissue that comprised the heart and scroll ivy. The morbid etchings visible on his outer arms and over his collarbone stood in vivid contrast to his pale skin. An audible gasp came from a female reporter close enough to the stage to see the scars in detail.

"The FBI has requested that due to my personal experience with the subject I assist in the investigation. To that end, the following information may help protect the public at large. Miller has a specific type he'll try to acquire. If you are a gay man, blond, five foot eight to six foot tall, and have a lean, athletic build, please do not travel by car alone and do not accept or give help to strangers while on the road. With one exception, Miller somehow took all his victims from their vehicles. The location varied, but the one constant was that the victim was traveling alone. Stuart Miller is intelligent, and while he may not appear dangerous, he has successfully trapped, tortured and killed twelve strong, resourceful men. Do not underestimate this man. I'm told a picture of Miller is being superimposed on this video feed in addition to the tip line number for anyone to report seeing him. Please, if you believe you see Miller—or think you have —call in. The FBI continues to work with local law enforcement to locate and apprehend Stuart Miller. At this time, we ask for everyone's cooperation as we move forward with this active investigation. Thank you."

A cascading roar of shouting voices lifted at once. Liam heard his name yelled by the woman in the front row. "Agent Mercier, what could you possibly hope to gain by appearing at this press conference?"

Liam stopped and directed his stare at the woman. Steele grabbed his arm and pulled him toward the exit, but Liam twisted his arm out of Steele's grip.

"What could I hope to gain? Was that your question?" The woman nodded and the crowd quieted.

"Miller made me a promise. He repeated his pledge to me with every twisted cut he carved into my body. Thirteen days of unbelievable pain and torture, yet he made me one promise. I would be his last victim. He made that oath based on the fact that he would complete his ritual, kill me and it would be over. He failed. Because I didn't die, someone else may. So what do I hope to gain? I don't know, lady. Maybe I gain the peace of mind that at least I tried to save another human from enduring the twisted, sick things Miller will put him through."

Steele grabbed Liam's discarded hoodie and slid up to the microphones. "Thank you. There will be no more questions accepted." Liam allowed himself to be pointed toward the exit and Steele escorted him from the barrage of questions being shouted at him.

The door to the side of the press conference area opened and they immediately ducked into a small room. An agent wearing a long-haired blond wig and dressed in the same clothes as Liam slipped Liam's sweatshirt over his head, pulled up the hood and exited the room flanked by another four agents. Once they were safely out, Liam let out a lungful of air.

"We couldn't have scripted her question any better. If they broadcast that, he'll react."

Liam's silent agreement must have concerned Steele because he moved closer. Liam could feel the man's heat through his thin T-shirt.

"Are you all right? How do you feel?" Steele pulled Liam's back against his hard chest. The agent wrapped him in warmth.

Liam let himself relax into the cocoon of strength encircling him. "Believe it or not, I'm doing okay. Relieved that portion is over. I don't know why, but I don't have that sickening feeling running just beneath my skin." Liam turned in Steele's arms. "I take that back. I do know why. I knew you were here. It made a difference."

Steele lowered his head, the man's lips hovering over Liam's. "I want to be here for you. This feels right." The warmth of Steele's breath caressed Liam's skin. Their eyes locked, each searching for something. Liam wanted to believe Steele could see what he felt. He needed the man to know how deep his emotions ran. He could say it, but something stopped the words.

Liam broke the moment when he lifted and pressed his lips against Steele's. The tender, reassuring contact ended too soon for Liam's liking. A noise from outside the partitioned area grew louder before it ebbed. The laughter of numerous people drifted away. Liam dropped his head against Steele's shoulder for a moment before he pulled away and put a respectable amount of space between them.

"You didn't have to pull away." Steele put both hands in his pockets, displaying the tent in the front of his slacks. Steele's eyebrows waggled when Liam shifted his gaze from the man's impressive bulge to his face.

Liam muffled a small laugh. His own cock raged behind the jeans he'd worn. A rather bizarre thought struck him. He was happy and warm. He had never believed he would be able to feel like this again. "I know, and I'm sorry. I still have a hard time trusting that this won't backfire. I'm gun-shy." Liam leaned against the wall and crossed his arms over his chest.

Steele adopted a similar position on the opposite wall. "I understand that. We'll go at your pace. But you need to know I've fought too damn hard to be who I am to hide."

"I don't want you to hide, but I'm not sure I'll ever be ready for public displays." Liam looked down at his Chucks and shrugged. He'd never been overt with his sexual tendencies or relationships before Miller. Being that way now? His reaction wasn't a reflection of his feelings for Steele. It was an ingrained survival technique.

Steele pushed off from the wall and stalked across the room. He placed his hands on either side of Liam's head. "I can deal with that, but if I want to kiss you"—Steele dipped his head and brushed his lips against Liam's—"I'll kiss you and you'll let me."

"Will I?" Liam knew he would, but he wanted Steele to work for it.

Steele's chest rumbled under Liam's hand when he laughed. "Yeah, you will, and you'll like it too."

"Really? What makes you think that?" Liam couldn't help the smile that played at his lips. It had been so damn long since he'd felt light and carefree. Even with Miller lurking in the background, the connection he felt with Steele eclipsed the fear.

"You're killing my confidence here, Liam. Tell me you don't like it and I'll stop." Steele dipped his head and sipped at Liam's lips, never giving more than teasing caresses.

Liam groaned and pushed Steele away. "Stop teasing me or I'll end up coming in my pants. How does that work for your confidence?"

Steele lifted that damn eyebrow again. Someday Liam was going to tell him how fucking sexy that movement was to him. Maybe—or maybe not. Steele wasn't hurting in the ego arena. Didn't want to give the man too big of a head.

The agent smirked and leaned against the partition. He rubbed the back of his neck and glued his stare to the ceiling as he spoke. "Okay, so back to the case. Miller now knows for sure you're working with us. If he hasn't collected all his supplies and a location, he'll be enticed to finish getting them now. We're monitoring every source for medical equipment we can. We've identified vacant warehouses in our sphere of observation with the refrigeration units he needs. We've warned his potential victim pool and we're monitoring all missing persons cases meeting Miller's criteria. Hopefully the new push with the media will give us something."

Liam nodded, the mention of the case and Miller killing any lingering desires the agent induced. "And now we wait. If something doesn't give, I'll need to be seen. And I'll need to be alone." A shiver of apprehension climbed up his spine. Abruptly changing the subject before he could get sucked down the rabbit hole, Liam asked, "Has Masterson gotten back to you yet?"

Steele shook his head. "No, but I'll give him an hour or so more to work the scene and interview the people who reported the discovery. Once this place clears out some, we'll head back to the safe house. Hardin and Fleming will ghost us to make sure no one is trailing us there. We should be clear soon. Hopefully anyone wanting more on the story followed them out."

"Yeah, but tell that agent I want my hoodie back. It's Phil's favorite."

CHAPTER 14

"*S*ee anything?" Steele scanned the rear-views again. They'd taken an indirect route back to the estate.

"Nah, we're clear." Hardin's voice traveled over the vehicle's internal speaker. "Want us to go get something for dinner? Fleming's been bitching that she's hungry."

"You fucking liar! I'm so kicking your ass. I ain't said shit, chief. This whiner has been grouching about needing food and for once, I agree. He's puny. Wouldn't last a day in the hood." Fleming's heavily accented voice pulled a smile from both Steele and Liam.

"Yeah, go ahead. We'll head to the house. If you're getting Italian, don't forget—"

"Masterson doesn't like peppers. We know." Hardin and Fleming's voices sounded as one.

"Yeah, well, you forgot last time and I had to put up with his bitching for a week." Steele hit the button on the steering wheel that ended the conversation before his team's comments could follow.

"He hasn't checked in yet?" Liam's question mirrored his own internal thoughts.

"No. I'm going to give him thirty more minutes before I contact him. This was a routine call. Maybe he got caught in traffic. I-95 is a bitch, no matter what time of day you're driving." Steele had faith in Masterson. He was a damn good agent and the locals had held both the truck and driver. Steele had no logical reason to be concerned. He was probably just on edge because Miller was a fucking wild card. Thinking you knew what he'd do was an advantage—for Miller.

Steele pulled up to the wrought iron gates and rolled down his window. As he punched in the access code, his phone vibrated. Masterson's name lit up the display. He hit the steering wheel button to accept the call.

"Where in the hell have you been? I expected a call hours ago." Steele hated being a stickler for protocol, but Sam was diligent and the deviation was unlike him. He'd have a good excuse, but Steele was still going to bust his balls. Just because he could.

"Forgive me. I did so try to hurry, but your agent was... difficult to obtain information from." Liam's hand gripped Steele's arm like a vise. He knew. Liam didn't need to identify the voice. He'd heard enough of the taped voice to recognize Miller.

"You better not have hurt him, you son of a bitch. I'll—" Steele slammed the car into park and picked up his phone. He hit a series of buttons trapping the call and initiating a trace.

"You'll do nothing. If you want your man back in... well, almost one piece, you'd be wise to do your homework. Tell Liam I saw him. Not live, mind you. I was busy convincing your man to cooperate, but the news has been magnificent about broadcasting his beautiful face. You want your agent. I want Liam. I'll trade."

"I don't have that authority and I don't have Liam. He's

been moved to a secure location."

"Really? It's a shame your agent isn't my type. He'll probably bleed out anyway after the beating he's taken. It's a pity. Your agent isn't the restful type. I remember Liam enjoyed this view with me. I wonder if your agent will? Some people don't like the way things must be. Orion's belt calls to Liam and to me. Clock's ticking, Agent McKenzie. Got to hang up and take out the battery before your trace narrows my location. I'll call back—maybe."

The line clicked dead and Steele grabbed for Liam and his phone in the same movement. The smaller man's body was ice cold. The shock of hearing Miller's voice had sent him into a panic-induced anxiety attack. Steele pulled Liam to him, slammed the car into gear and drove as he dialed.

"Hey, chief, did you change—"

"Miller has Sam. Get your asses back here. Stat." Steele disconnected and called his supervisor. The conversation lasted less than a minute, and that's all it took for Steele to get Liam to the front door of the house. Steele pocketed the phone and held his lover up. Fuck, Liam was heavier than he looked. Steele somehow managed to make it inside.

He stood in front of Liam and put both hands on the smaller man's face, making Liam look at him. "You have got to stay with me, Liam. I need you now like I've never needed anyone before. That bastard has my partner. If he hasn't killed him yet, he will. Please stay with me. Help me get this fucker."

Liam nodded, but his eyes bounced from object to object in the room. In his gut, Steele knew Liam hadn't heard a word he'd said. Damn it, he needed the man to focus. Desperate to get Liam's attention, Steele did the only thing that came to mind. He reached back and bitch-slapped Liam—hard.

Liam's doubled up right fist caught Steele's jaw. Steele

staggered back but was able to deflect the follow-up left uppercut. He wrapped up Liam's arm and twisted it behind his back, forcing him into the wall. "Stop! Hey, it's me... Liam... it's me, Steele." Liam's unexpected punch was a wake-up call. *Son of a bitch,* his lover had one hell of a right hook.

"Fuck, let me go!" Liam ground out the words.

"I will. Just calm down." Steele leaned his body weight into Liam. "I need you to be here. Now. I need help to find Masterson."

"Orion's belt." Son of a bitch. Liam was still out of it.

"Come on, angel. You've got to pull it together for me." Steele relaxed his grip on Liam's arm and put his hand around the man's waist.

"What did he say about Orion's belt?" Liam's question came between panted breaths.

"Fuck... ahh... Orion's belt calls to you and to him. Why? What does that mean?" Steele pulled Liam away from the wall and turned him, desperate to see if the man was coherent.

Liam curled in on himself and slid down the wall. Steele lifted his hand to wipe a trickle of blood from the corner of his mouth. He watched as Liam seemed to disappear into his thoughts.

The shock and trauma tore through his lover. Steele had to lean in to hear his whisper. "At night Miller would turn off the light he used to work on me. I could see the stars through the skylight. He kept my table under it. He'd lay his head next to mine. He'd tell me..."

Steele crouched down and cupped Liam's cheek. Tears left trails of moisture down his lover's cheek. "He said things, talked to me like I was his... He loved the stars. It was the only time he wasn't hurting me, Steele. He's going to... Unless he has a new warehouse with a skylight, he's taken Masterson to the warehouse where I was found."

∽

LIAM WATCHED THROUGH A FOG. His shocked and terrified mind captured glimpses of events as they unfolded—Hardin and Fleming at the conference table, Steele's supervisor on one phone, Steele on the other, the FBI's HRT team on video link, several state police officers in uniform, and the agents geared up with tactical vests and radios. The breakthroughs of reality seemed to be freeze-framed, disjointed and foreign.

Liam drew a breath and forced himself to concentrate. Steele caught his supervisor by the arm and spoke in a hushed tone. Liam watched from the corner of the room. He glanced around him. He was in the right hand corner of the room. Just to the side of the door. His field of vision was unobstructed, but nobody noticed him because Liam hadn't moved. He couldn't. Not that it mattered. He didn't belong in the orchestrated dance that unfolded before him. He was five years away from the fight, and realistically it could have been a millennium. He didn't belong with the agents who were gearing up. His issues made him a liability. Masterson was probably dead because of him. Miller wouldn't stop. Liam had taunted him. *Mistake.* Miller was coming for him to complete his rituals. There wasn't anything he could do.

"Liam, angel, are you with me?" Liam physically jumped. Steele was right in front of him. He didn't remember seeing him cross the room.

"Hey, I've got to go. I'm leaving uniforms outside the house. I'll call you as soon as I can. Will you be okay?" The pity in Steele's eyes killed Liam. And at that moment Liam knew in his heart there could never be a future with Steele. Liam knew what he should do. The sharp reality of his course of action became as apparent as the ten-inch block lettering on Steele's tactical vest.

"Yeah, I'm fine. Go, get Masterson." Liam reached up and

touched Steele's stubbled cheek, committing the sensation to memory.

"I'll get him and we'll get Miller. I'll make this right." Steele grasped the back of Liam's neck and pulled him forward. The heat of his palm and lips seared into Liam's mind.

When Steele released him, Liam tried to smile. He wasn't sure if he'd succeeded. "Be safe and take care of yourself, Steele. Thank you."

Steele's concern showed in his eyes and the way he paused when he stood. He lifted Liam's chin and brushed his thumb across Liam's lips. "Everything will be all right, angel. I'll get him."

Liam swallowed hard and nodded. "I know you will, Steele. I'm sure of it." Liam drew a deep breath. "Goodbye."

Steele cocked his head and regarded Liam with a quizzical look. A member of the tactical assault team called to him and he stepped away. The worried glance over his shoulder hit Liam like a fist. Absolute silence surrounded him. Liam remained unmoving and waited.

The events of the night pounded through Liam's thoughts, and for once he didn't try to stop the fall into the rabbit hole. He knew where it would lead and still he dropped. He was tired of fighting, and after all, the end was inevitable. His mind slipped over the crest and he fell into the pull of the hell he'd kept at bay for so long. Over and over thoughts repeated. Torture. Pain. Miller's face. The call from the truck stop. Masterson's response. Pain and blinding light. The fear. His news conference. The wait for the building to clear. Miller's face. The soft hum of Miller's voice as he cut. Miller's phone call. Pain. Fear. Like an old-fashioned news-reel, Liam played the pictures on a loop that became faster and more condensed. The sea of faces in the news confer-ence. The agents, the reporters, the cameramen and technicians who put the mics up. Stars. Blinding light. Steele, Fleming, Hardin and Masterson. Miller. His mind flashed faster and faster until only Miller remained. Miller. His face thinner, his hair longer. Miller standing in front of him, watching him. Miller crossing the room. Miller. Then nothing. Blessed nothing.

CHAPTER 15

"McKenzie, thermals show maybe two people in the anteroom. It's the second office to the right as you breach the warehouse. There is a heat signature either crouched or sitting to the immediate right of the door, another across the room." Steele acknowledged the information and glanced over at Hardin and Fleming. They nodded that they had heard the HRT leader's comment.

"We are prepared to breach the main doors. My men will enter, clear and secure the area, and establish a perimeter. Your team processes it after we've cleared it. The entry into the office will be with flash bangs. Keep your asses glued to my entry team when we go in. We'll go hot, locked and loaded." Steele's team had done this before, and with this team. They all knew the drill. Usually the outcome wasn't favorable. Dealing with sick, sadistic killers… They all knew the odds of finding a hostage alive. Sometimes they got lucky. That was what he focused on now.

"Roger that. Be advised the perp is known for taking refuge in the right hand corner closest to the door." Steele's whispered warning was acknowledged. On a silent cue, the hostage rescue team advanced on the warehouse. The spring night was quiet except for the thrum of an occasional car that made its way across the transom bridge about a mile or so away. The normal sounds of the night, crickets, night birds and the scuffle of small animals through the overgrown underbrush surrounding the building, were conspicuously silent, as if nature was watching the events unfold. Steele tracked the breach and as soon as the last member of the team entered the facility he motioned to his team to advance. Fleming and Harding were hard on his six as he advanced through the warehouse door. Because of the advanced technology night vision goggles the team wore, the darkness played little or no part in the plan. The HRT sliced through the cavernous open bay, clearing the facility.

At the team lead's signal, Steele brought his agents forward. The hushed silence of the massive building was disturbed only by the faint shuffle of feet and the thunderous sound of Steele's heart as it slammed against his ribs. Masterson was behind that door. If the thermal had found him, he was still warm. Warm didn't mean alive, but Steele was clinging to hope. He had to... *Sam, damn it, you had better be alive.*

Once his team had tucked up behind the entry team, all hell busted loose. The door disappeared with one heaved thrust of the hand-held battering ram. The tossed flash-bang exploded at almost the exact same second it launched. The pressure switch trigger, apparently set to zero, activated as soon as it was thrown into the room.

Steele couldn't hear shit, but the man in front of him moved in a dance coordinated to perfection as the entry team poured through the door. Each member sighted his weapon on a specific point. In a coordinated sweep, they located the people in the room. Steele's gun leveled on the man in the corner of the room. His hands trembled in rage.

The bastard. The sadistic son of a bitch. Steele lunged toward the man.

"Sam! Damn it, don't move, and stop struggling. I got you. You're safe. Someone get me a fucking knife!" Steele holstered his weapon and carefully pulled the thick wire away from Masterson's windpipe. A fraction of an inch was all he could gain, but the gasp coming from his partner gave him hope. The man's face had been almost obliterated by blood and bruising. Miller had beaten the hell out of Masterson. Hardin arrived with wire cutters that he'd liberated from one of the entry team.

Steele held up Masterson as Hardin continued to cut away the wire that held him in his position beside the door.

"Miller? Did we get Miller?" Steele shouted the question.

"Negative. The other one is gone. Dead, but not long. Neck sliced. Poor bastard bled out." Fleming flashed a picture she'd taken of the victim. The man was the same size and color as Liam. The fucker had taken someone, but either Masterson had stumbled into something or Liam's appearance on television had changed Miller's course of action.

EMTs swarmed Masterson. The man's hands had been mangled. Steele cast a glance around the room. In the corner to the right of the table where the young man had bled out was a ballpeen hammer. Steele motioned toward Fleming. She immediately started to preserve the evidence.

Masterson's gasping, blood-filled cough pulled his attention back to his partner. He raised an abused hand and pointed toward Steele. Steele dropped to his knee immediately and tried to settle Masterson. "It's okay, Sam. We got you."

Steele's partner coughed as he ground out one word. "Liam."

"Liam is back at the safe house. I left uniforms. No

worries." Steele nodded to the EMT, who tried to put an oxygen mask over Masterson's deformed face.

"No! Miller... Help... Liam..."

Every molecule in Steele's body froze, then squeezed in an incomprehensible fear. "Miller knows where Liam is?"

Masterson managed a nod, and that was all it took for Steele to launch out of the office. He grabbed the HRT team lead and both men ran out of the building.

CHAPTER 16

"What the fuck do you mean we have nothing?" Steele threw his coffee cup against the wall, shattering the pottery against a row of binders holding policy letters, interoffice memos and directives. His office had become a fucking cage. "It's been eight hours! That motherfucker has Liam. He has to be close."

Hardin bent down and started to pick up the shards of ceramic. Fleming shook her head. "Chief, I was just coming to tell you we got a call from Miller's shrink, Dr. Sands. Evidently, he got back from his extended honeymoon last night. He wants a sit-down."

"Why the fuck isn't he here now, then?" Steele hadn't slept. He was living on stress and pure unadulterated hatred. Miller was a dead man. Steele had made a solemn vow he'd kill the son of a bitch. Masterson was fighting for his life and Liam—Oh dear God... Liam. Steele scrubbed his face with both hands and bit back the surge of emotions that drove him nearly insane. He knew what Liam was going through and he couldn't—

"He should be here in a half hour or so, depending on

traffic. I told him to get here as fast as he could." Fleming pulled her laptop bag closer to her body and glanced at Hardin. "Ah, can I get us some more coffee?"

Steele ran his hands through his hair and groaned, ignoring the question. "Okay, there has to be something we're missing."

Hardin dumped pieces of the fractured cup into the garbage can. "I'll call the hospital again, but the charge nurse said they didn't anticipate Sam being out of surgery for another hour or two. They have to reconstruct his face."

Nobody spoke. They all knew Masterson hadn't been given great odds. The work the surgeons were doing now was to clear his airways and prevent any shattered bones from doing more damage. And that was a joke. Sam would never look the same again. They'd left a team at the hospital, but Steele still had Hardin calling every half hour for an update.

"Masterson won't be able to help us. Where would this bastard hide?"

Fleming's question lifted Steele's head. A thought struck him and he held up his hand to silence Hardin's response. "What if he isn't hiding? What if he is in plain sight? Look at the area. In the fifty-mile radius, we have what... a couple hundred medical facilities, if you count offices and clinics?"

"What's he going to do? Waltz into a doctor's office and take up residency? Wouldn't that be just a little suspicious?" Hardin's question plucked the straws Steele had been grasping out of his hand. A knock at the door had all three of them swiveling their heads.

"Hey, excuse me. I'm looking for an Agent Fleming or McKenzie. The guys downstairs who gave me a cavity search before they let me in said this was the office?"

"Who are you?" Steele wasn't in the mood for jokes or jokers.

"Dr. Tony Sands. I was Miller's therapist for the last five years."

McKenzie strode across the room and extended his hand. "SSA McKenzie, this is Agent Fleming and Agent Hardin. Angela said you might have some information?" Steele motioned toward the chair in front of his desk and the doc plopped down. Fleming and Hardin leaned against the bureau to the left of Steele's desk.

"Information? Maybe, but I definitely have his background, motivation and intent. Since my visits were court-ordered I can legally divulge information to you."

Steele sat behind his desk and steepled his fingers, trying to calm himself enough to ask intelligent questions. "Doc, he's got Liam. He damn near killed my partner and he's in the wind. What can you give me to work with?"

"Liam is his fixation. If it's any consolation, I don't think he'll kill the man... at least not right away. Although he never once said why, he believes Liam is his fiancé, or at least God's replacement for his fiancé."

Steele held up his hand. "What fiancé?"

Doc Sands leaned forward, resting his forearms on his knees. "Getting anything from Miller was a tit-for-tat conversation. He's manipulative, obsessive, and lives in a world none of us will ever be able to comprehend. His extreme intelligence complicates even the simplest treatment protocols. Even medicated to the point he was, the man is smarter than ninety-five percent of the population. I believe there was a psychotic break that occurred in college—medical school, to be exact. What I know is also bolstered with five years' worth of... well, for the lack of a better term, my gut feelings."

Steele leaned over his desk blotter to emphasize his words. "Doc, that man has taken Liam. Anything you can give me will help. I'll take your gut feelings and any other information you can provide."

Doc Sands swallowed hard and peered up at the ceiling for a moment before he leveled his gaze at Steele. "The indications are he first presented symptoms in medical school. In Miller's sessions, he refused to talk about his early childhood years. He once stated he didn't start to live until he met his first love. The man, Whitney—I don't know if that was the man's first name or last, was his life. Miller told me he knew this Whitney fellow was in love with him. That's all I have after five years, but I know Whitney left medical school and Miller followed him. The length of time he was with his first love—Miller's words, not mine—has some significance to him. I checked the police reports and according to what I could discern he was gone fourteen months almost to the day. Miller's a sociopath *but* he has fixated on Mr. Mercier and that may give you some time. From what I have heard about what happened to the doctor who filled in for me... I'm sure Miller has escalated."

"Yeah, Doc, we deduced the same thing. So what you're telling me is we aren't dealing with the same psychotic who ritualistically killed twelve men."

"Thirteen," the doctor answered immediately.

"Excuse me?" Steele sat ramrod straight in his seat.

"Thirteen. Whitney was his first—or at least I believe he was. I have nothing but my gut to base that assumption on, but after five years, Miller never said anything that would lead me to believe I was incorrect in my assumption. Miller believes your agent is his gift from God. He is the ritualistic fourteenth."

Fleming adjusted her position against the credenza and shuddered. "Damn, Doc, how in the hell can you deal with people like him day after day? At least all we have to do is catch them."

"Honestly, I'm burned out. I've given the staff at the hospital notice. I've bought into an existing mental health and physical rehab practice. We're renovating a building just west of here. I'm going to switch sides and start helping the victims of violent crime instead of the criminals."

"Hey, Doc?" Steele's voice interrupted the side conversation. "Did you tell Miller about your wedding? The date?"

Sands nodded. "Yeah, like I said, our conversations were tit for tat. I gave him tidbits of information about me or what was going on in my life, generic and harmless, and he gave me pieces of information about his past or his crimes."

"Did he know you were leaving the hospital?"

"I don't know. I didn't tell him, but the staff talk to each other when patients are around. As you can imagine, a lot of the patients are heavily medicated, so a quick conversation with another employee could be the only intelligent interaction a person could get for hours. Why?"

"Just putting some pieces of the puzzle together. Did Miller ever get aggressive with you?"

"No. I think our conversations were the highlight of his week. The orderlies made comments over the years that Miller seemed to anticipate our sessions. Most likely he enjoyed the mental stimulation. Each week at the conclusion of the interview, I'd give him a riddle. When he returned the next week, he'd have the answer."

"So he liked you?" Hardin asked.

"No, he tolerated me. Honestly, it felt more like he played me. He is the reason I'm leaving the hospital."

"Doc, if you had to guess, where would Miller take Liam?" Steele was grasping at straws, but if the man had any idea... Hell, it couldn't hurt.

"I couldn't begin to know. He's obsessive. His ritualistic compulsions drove him to the site he picked last time. I'm not sure if he'll repeat the ritual or just finish what he'd planned originally. Hell, he's impossible to predict, but he'll probably drug his victim. Miller said he loved the peace of the drugged victim. He fed on the emotion in their eyes when he tortured them. Honestly, he could be anywhere. He's too damn smart to make the same mistake that led the FBI to him the first time. The man gets off on being smarter than anyone else. It gave him no end of joy to know the other team had cast a nationwide search for him and he was less than a quarter mile from where he'd taken his first victim. He gets—hell, I don't know—maybe a manic energy from flaunting his superiority over us lesser mortals. I'm sorry I don't know where he'd take your man."

The phone on Steele's desk barely rang once before he had the receiver in his hand and ground out his name.

"Agent McKenzie, the local PD got an anonymous tip. They found Caleb James—dead. And sir? The police chief thinks it was Miller."

CHAPTER 17

Steele lifted the black plastic flap covering the body. Repulsed, he drew back and momentarily closed his eyes. The coroner gave him a sideways glance. He didn't recognize the medical examiner; obviously, she was one he'd never worked with before. He pulled his badge and flashed it as he walked over to the petite redhead.

"SSA McKenzie. I need you to give me a rundown on your preliminaries." Steele lifted a hand and beckoned Hardin from where he stood talking with the responding patrol.

The woman placed her pen in the clamp of her clipboard and turned to face them. She took a deep breath and shook her head. "I've only been doing this job for three years, but I doubt I'll ever see anything more appalling. Starting with physical damage… The man bled out. But I'm not sure if that was before or after he was castrated."

"Miller cut his balls off?" Hardin's shocked inquiry said the words Steele was thinking.

"I don't know who did it, and no, what happened was just a simple dissection. The man's scrotum was cut open, his testes were pushed out, and from the remains I found, the organs were pulled out. Due to the amount of blood loss I found... Well, it appears to have happened before he died. Due to the lack of blood loss associated with the words carved into his dermis, I'd say that happened after he died.

"What words?" Steele lifted the black plastic again.

The coroner squatted down and rolled Caleb James' body. The block lettering in the man's flesh froze the blood in Steele's veins.

The end of Liam's suffering is nearer than you think.

"What the fuck?" Hardin's question brought Steele's eyes away from the corpse.

"The bastard is taunting us." Fleming's comment as she walked up echoed Steele's own thoughts.

"How long has he been dead?" Steele asked the coroner.

"Based on liver temp and the ambient temperature here in the warehouse, along with the settling of the bodily fluids and rigor, I'd say anywhere from eight to twelve hours. I'll need to check that, but it's a ballpark."

"So he couldn't have had James and Masterson at the same time?" A shudder ran through Hardin.

Steele put his hand on the man's shoulder and squeezed. "Whatever happened, the fact remains Sam is still alive and fighting. He'll make it because he's a survivor." Steele had to believe it. He had to or he'd lose it. The two men closest to him—his partner and his lover—had been taken by that sick fuck. He had to believe both would survive, and he'd do anything he could to make sure it happened.

"Fleming, get the forensics crew working. I want evidence logged and on my phone as soon as it's processed. If he had Sam or Liam here, I need to know."

"Roger that, chief."

He turned to Hardin and nodded toward the rent-a-cop that had responded to the report of a suspicious person. The vacant storefront was less than five miles from where they'd found Masterson.

Steele watched Hardin as he headed to interview the witness. Steele scanned the backroom of the small, vacant store. The old workbench seemed to be painted a cinnamon brown from the amount of Caleb James' blood that covered it. Two scalpels lay on the floor, both covered with smeared blood. Steele pulled back, not physically, but mentally. Now that he'd seen what was at the crime scene, what wasn't there was troubling him. No clothes. James was naked. So either the man had been transported here naked or Miller had taken his clothes. But why? How could he get James to this location? Steele exited the rear of the building. The alley at both ends of the block had been taped off and beat cops contained the scene.

Steele pulled his LED flashlight out and started a strip and grid search of the area, beginning with the real estate closest to the back door. Steele headed toward three double-topped dumpsters. Steele's eyes watered from the stench of the garbage. He pulled a handkerchief out of his coat pocket and covered his mouth. He only carried the damn thing as a breathing filter, but it had seen more than enough use. The first two dumpsters were a bust, nothing but stench. Emptied recently, the bins were lined only with the sticky residue of rancid fluids. The third was a goldmine. Caleb's clothes and —from what Steele could see—his wallet and cell phone. He removed the handkerchief from his mouth and let out a piercing whistle. Two uniformed patrolmen hustled to his location. He sent one after Fleming and had the other stand guard until a forensic technician could clear the evidence site.

"Here you go, chief." Fleming handed him the phone. "It's been dusted and all latents have been lifted."

Steele hit a button on the old phone and thanked his

lucky stars James hadn't password protected it. Steele swiped back to the main screen and hit the text message icon. There was only one. It instructed James to meet behind the store where they'd just found his body. The last lines of the text explained why the man had come without following protocol.

If you bring in anyone, I will kill not one, but two, men and their deaths will be on your hands.

The man was already eaten up with guilt. He'd felt responsible for Liam's capture the first time. And he was. No doubt about it. The overwhelming guilt the man lived with had become the thing that Miller had used to lure him to his death. Steele gazed unseeingly down the alley. One question kept running through his mind. Why would Miller go after James? The pieces to the puzzle were not adding up. Miller wasn't showing ritualistic tendencies. He was slaughtering people. People who...*shit*. People who'd prevented him from getting to Liam.

CHAPTER 18

Steele pulled up in front of the safe house. His body ached, his head hurt and it didn't help that he was past exhausted. Liam was in the hands of that maniac. He'd work until he collapsed. What he was enduring couldn't be compared to what Liam was living through. God, Steele prayed Liam was still living. His team needed an answer to his prayers right now. They'd chased every conceivable combination of leads and come up empty.

Steele's eyes wandered to the front door of the house. The bastard had walked through that door and just taken Liam. How? The patrol he'd left hadn't seen or heard a thing. There had been no sign of a struggle, no indication of forced entry. Liam was just gone. A vehicle pulled up beside him. He glanced over and huffed out a lungful of air. Hardin and Fleming. Those two were fucking rocks he could stand on. Steele got out of the vehicle at the same time as his agents.

"Thought I told you to get some rest." Steele's comment was meant to be gruff, but it came out more like a yawn.

"Yeah, well, we'll rest when you do." Fleming flipped the

response for both of them. Damn Jersey stubbornness. Grateful for the support, he made it up the steps and into the hall. Steele froze as Phil trotted down the hall. The beast wrapped itself around his legs and purred. Okay…even the cat knew something was wrong. Risking getting his hand sliced off, Steele reached down and pet the damn thing. Phil pushed into his hand and trilled up at him.

"Yeah, buddy, I know. We'll find him. I promise." Steele straightened and shrugged off his suit jacket as he made it into the library. He walked straight to the whiteboard and wiped it clean.

"Okay, on the drive over—or when I was sitting in front of the house, I'm not really sure which—it came to me that we need to take another angle on this. Not macro, but micro. Macro is Miller's past, his psychology, his murders that happened prior to these events. We've screwed away the last twenty hours of the critical first forty-eight. I'm saying fuck that. Fuck all of it. Wipe it out of the picture, because it's noise. Let's focus on Liam's abduction. What do we know?"

Steele faced the board. He scribbled *no break-in.* Fleming stood and walked to the board. "No offense, chief, but I can't read that shit. I got this." She wiped the squiggly lines out and looked at him questioningly.

"No break-in. No signs of forced entry. No vehicle seen or heard." Steele listed the items.

"No tire tracks or turn-around points indicated in the lawn beyond the hill or the front of the mansion. Miller didn't leave fingerprints," Hardin added to the list.

Steele grunted and added, "That's easy. Gloves." Latex. Steele tacked that one on mentally.

"We've all seen Liam lose his shit, chief. What was going on with him right before we left?" Fleming asked.

"He was barely keeping it together. I hated leaving him,

but he assured me he'd be okay." Steele's gut clenched again. The guilt of leaving Liam tore at his heart. He should have assumed Masterson had broken, but fuck, the thought had never crossed his mind. Steele had let Miller take Liam, the one thing he'd promised to prevent.

"Okay, so how could Miller get into the house, find Liam, and leave with him without being detected?" Hardin asked. The question brought energy to the brainstorming session.

"Where was patrol?" Fleming wrote both her and Hardin's questions on the board.

"According to their statements..." Hardin flipped his finger across the screen of his tablet a couple times. "They were sitting at the southeast corner of the house. They saw no movement. The lights did not go on or off as would indicate Liam moved around the house, so let's assume he stayed in the library where the chief left him."

Steele nodded and jolted when Phil jumped into his lap. The cat pushed into Steele and curled into his lap purring. Damn, the world was truly on its ear right now. Fucking ninja cat from hell was making nice. Steele drew his hand across the cat's fur. If he didn't find Liam soon—

"Okay, so how can you get into and out of this house without anyone seeing you if they are sitting over there?"

"If we—" The front door of the house slammed open. Phil became a long-haired projectile that launched as Steele flew out of his seat and drew his weapon. Within two seconds all three agents' weapons were trained on the open library door. Steele braced for action, his heart pounding as adrenaline coursed through his body. A huge man wearing torn jeans, a sleeveless Whitesnake T-shirt and an armful of leather bracelets practically ran through the door but skidded to an immediate stop and raised his hands.

"Dude, lower the fucking iron. I own this place." Steele's

mind took a couple of seconds to place the familiar face. Lucifer. The billionaire rock-fucking-legend stood in all his six-foot-eight-inch glory not ten feet from his team.

Steele released the grip he had on his .45 and lowered his weapon at about the same time as Hardin and Fleming.

"You're FBI? Where's Sam? Is he okay? I got a call from the head of my estate saying that he was hurt. He hasn't answered his phone. I've been going insane, man." The rocker's chest heaved and the emotion in his eyes told Steele exactly what Masterson wouldn't reveal.

Steele grasped the back of his neck and rubbed it, trying to calm down. "He's just out of surgery. They have him in the ICU. His condition is critical. The fucker we're tracking tore him up. The floor he's on is locked down until we catch this guy. You'll need an escort to get in."

"What the fuck are we waiting for? I flew back from Stuttgart the second I heard he'd been injured. Please, man, you got to get me in to see him." The mismatched brown and blue eyes that bolstered the rocker's recognition factor begged for help as much as his words.

"We got you, man. Fleming? Could you drive him? Get him up to see Masterson and do a status check for us? We'll be here working the angles." Steele watched her back straighten and he knew she wanted to object, but the rocker swung his desperate look at her and she folded.

"Yeah, I can do that, chief." She grabbed her phone and headed out the door.

"Thanks. I just got to know for myself that he's okay. You know what I mean?" Steele put two and two together and realized Lucifer fucking Cross was the man Sam loved—loved and gave up. Fuck. His mind snapped to Liam. Steele couldn't give up. He wouldn't. Steele forced back the emotion that boiled just under his fragile veneer of control. He nodded. "Yeah, I know. Go… see your man."

A dazzling smile spread across the rocker's face right before he spun and took off after Fleming. Steele stared at the empty door. At least when Masterson woke up, he'd have someone who cared for him beside him—someone to help, to ease the pain and the fear of what the injuries might mean to his future. The pain of his own loss tore at Steele—angered him to the point of rage. He would make it his life's mission to hunt down Miller. Liam deserved that, even if Steele didn't get to him in time.

"Damn, he's way bigger than he looks in his videos." Hardin's voice brought Steele back to the present.

"Yeah. Where were we?" Steele focused on the whiteboard again.

"Looking for exits that the patrol wouldn't see parked at the southeast corner of the house."

Steele nodded and spoke. "Okay, so with the exception of the front door and the door to the pool, which can be seen from the patrol's position, that leaves the kitchen door and the door off the downstairs master bedroom. Let's go take a look."

Hardin was on Steele's heels. The master bedroom faced the gardens and had a five-foot privacy wall on three sides. If Miller wanted camouflage, that would be the entrance. Steele walked the patio and paced it out, looking for easy ingress or egress. A single man could get in, but taking someone out? Dead weight or at gunpoint? No, the terrain presented too many obstacles, too little control.

Steele headed to the kitchen. The staff used this entrance. The outside pathway was built using interlocking paver stones. The stones branched into several walkways—a direct path to the adjacent house about three hundred feet away, an offshoot to the running track and sports areas, and the largest pathway leading to the main house. Steele walked the stones looking for any disruption in the placement or indication of a struggle. Hardin's flashlight spotlighted where they walked, although the path lights and associated landscape lighting made the inspection easy to accomplish, even this late at night.

Steele stopped about halfway between the houses. This was the first point where a person could deviate from the path. Peat moss grew between huge stepping-stones that lead down toward the tennis courts, but there was no exit from the estate from that location and none of the delicate moss seemed to be disturbed.

"The forensics team did a complete sweep of all the exits and entrances, chief. There was no sign of forced entry."

"The kitchen door may not have been locked. That's the way the staff gains access to the house." Steele stopped and spun on his heel. "Have all the staff been accounted for? Did Miller have help?"

"Chief, I understand what you're saying, but slow down for a minute. You got the report. Everyone's accounted for, and Miller has never had a partner."

"That we know of."

"Granted. That we know about."

"How can we explain how Miller got in and out?" Steele snapped out in his frustration.

"Listen, chief... One thing we haven't looked at is that maybe—and I'm only saying this for the sake of argument— maybe Liam walked away on his own? Do you think all of this shit got to be too much for him and he just checked out? I mean, just the other day when you two got into it, he said he was leaving. Even though we were upstairs, your shouting match woke me up. Hell, we all heard it. Could he have just gone?"

Steele ran both hands through his hair and groaned. The thought had crossed his mind, but he'd summarily dismissed it. He continued down the path heading toward the other smaller house, looking for something—anything. "No. He wouldn't leave Phil for one, and he and I had—have—something. He wouldn't walk away. He knows Miller is after him and deep down he knows he's not emotionally able to deal with that alone. Liam is smarter than that."

Harden hopped in front of him and got in his face. "Right, but you said yourself the call from Miller freaked him the hell out. Have you talked to that doc again? Does she agree with you?" Hardin's quiet voice came almost hopeful. Like he wanted Liam to have just left?

"I don't give a flying fuck who agrees with me." Steele's rage pushed forward and so did he. He grabbed Hardin and pushed him against the door of the adjacent house they now stood beside. The latch gave and Steele landed on top of Hardin. Both men grunted when they hit the hardwood floor inside the door.

Hardin started to speak but Steele slapped his hand over the man's mouth. "These houses are supposed to be locked and mothballed while Lucifer's band is touring." His whisper brought a nod from Hardin. Steele carefully lifted off his agent, his gun drawn, then pointed into the interior of the kitchen. He lowered a hand toward Hardin but the man knocked it away, coming up with his service weapon in hand.

Steele nodded toward the left. The alarm panel flashed green. It had been bypassed into access. Wires hung from the panel—the green plastic-wrapped filament dangling while the white and black had been twisted together, short circuiting the entire system.

Steele flashed a hand signal for Hardin to call for backup. Hardin's eyes grew large and he mouthed, *wait for me*. Steele nodded and Hardin carefully stepped out of the house to place the call. Steele worked the layout of the room.

A muffled crash of something metal from somewhere in the bowels of the house drew Steele's attention. He carefully crossed the vast kitchen, taking cover behind the massive kitchen island. Hardin reappeared at the back door and Steele signaled for him to hold.

CHAPTER 19

*L*iam's mind migrated from a terror-filled nightmare to a waking hell. He couldn't move. A light bulb suspended close to his face blinded him to anything but the smallest amount of peripheral vision. To his right hung an IV. The drugs that froze his muscles dripped from the clear bag into the tube currently inserted in his vein. Liam rolled his eyes to the left. Nothing, until he heard it. Miller was here. Talking? But the sound was wrong. Tinny, from a distance.

"You are the one responsible. You took him from me and for that, you must be punished. I haven't quite decided how I'm going to do that. I need to get back to my slumbering masterpiece, so I guess expediency will determine my course of action."

Liam's mind raced. Get back to me?

"I'm disappointed, Mr. James. You should care for your team as much as Agent McKenzie cared for his. His rush to save his agent gave me exactly what I needed—a wide-open window of opportunity and the best hiding place in the world. I'm right under his nose and he'll never know it. Not until I let Liam die."

Miller had Caleb James? Liam tried to move again. His left leg twitched and his right hand moved a fraction of an inch. Liam heard a scrape of metal against metal and stopped his efforts. If Miller saw him move, he'd up the dose of medication.

The sound of a light object rolling across the floor seemed to move from his right to his left. He tracked the sound with his eyes and cringed internally when he heard the sound of liquid hitting a metal basin. He knew the sound intimately. The acidic smell of rubbing alcohol whiffed through the air, sending bile into Liam's throat. The pain of years past became fresh and poignant in his mind, as if he'd never been freed from Miller's torture.

"That agent I set up with the medical equipment heist was tough. Big guy, though, nothing like you, Agent James. You know, I think you could take a lesson from that agent. Did you know I had to crush every knuckle in his right hand before he even told me the security code to his phone? No? Well I did." Miller laughed. "Can you imagine what he endured when he tried to refuse to give up the safe house? You've heard how sensitive the nerves around the fingernails and toenails are, right? Admirable, really. He's such a strong, strong man. Well, he was. The man's own body weight was strangling him against a piano wire when I left. I think the wire was the C note? Not the high C, the lower C. The wire was thicker and able to hold his weight without killing him immediately. It was tricky trying to figure out what gauge of wire to use. I settled for one thin enough to cut through the skin and through the arteries in his neck if he passed out or McKenzie took too long to figure out my location. From the response time I saw...well, the chances of reaching him in time were slim. Even if he is rescued, he'll never be normal again. His face, you understand. I didn't like it, so I decided I'd help him rearrange a few things."

The sounds coming from the area to his left proved James hadn't been given the same cocktail currently dripping into Liam's arm. His quiet murmurs that begged Miller to stop only seemed to fuel the maniac's one-sided discussion.

"Hush now. I know this isn't pleasant, but you, Mr. James, are not a nice person. I may be psychotic— No, wait, that's not right. I *am* psychotic—clinically insane, actually. But even in my—how did my shrink put it? Oh, yes, my altered state of reality—I've risked everything to take care of my Liam. McKenzie risked the life of one of his team. Liam risked his life to call out to me on national television. Everyone has risked something—except you. You didn't do shit. And why was that? He was a member of your team. *Your* team, Mr. James, and yet you did absolutely nothing to find him, to help him. You know what I learned?" Miller's stage whisper continued. "You didn't come because he was gay."

A tsking sound preceded Miller's comments. "Simply being gay *isn't* a crime, Mr. James. But you still tried and convicted a person you were supposed to protect. You sentenced him to death, too. Not that you could have stopped me...*damn it!* If you'd come when you were supposed to, I'd have been able to mislead you yet again and finish my perfect lover, but oh no, you couldn't do anything you were supposed to do, could you? No, you didn't come and didn't come and didn't come, so I let my guard down. And you dragged your feet just because you wanted Liam dead. You did, didn't you?"

Liam heard the distant sound of James begging—incoherent babble pleading, imploring Miller to release him.

The sound of the voices he heard wasn't right. The small, tinny sounding... a recording?

"You weren't strong enough to stay true to your course of

action. And just as I was ready to set Liam free, you showed up and took him away."

James screamed, a high keening wail. The sound of the man's body thrashing, pulling on restraints, brought tears of frustration to Liam's eyes. He knew whatever Miller was doing was to punish him as much as James. "Oh yes…well, as you can tell, the skin here at the testes is sensitive. The scalpel is very sharp, and that little cut is precise, so your pain is still manageable. But we do need to keep this area clean so I can see as I work."

Liam expected the shriek of pain from James, but it didn't make it easier to hear. No one who hadn't lived through it had any idea how perverse Miller's torture could be.

"Am I going to have to get angry with you, Agent James? This simpering isn't conducive to my work. Severing the vocal chords is a risky cut. I could nick an artery and then you'd bleed out. I don't want that. Not yet. Soon. But guess what? I have a surprise for both you and my beautiful Liam. I've decided I'm keeping him until the drugs or my attentions push him over the edge. I decided I didn't need to finish him. You see, he is already my perfect lover."

Lost in his own gut-wrenching horror, Liam didn't hear James' mumbled response, but Miller thought whatever he'd said was funny. His insane laugh sounded around Liam. "Oh dear man, I haven't even started with you yet. Liam endured so much more. If you only knew. He is the perfect canvas. Now, where was I? Oh yes. Your castration."

Liam saw movement to his left. Miller came into view and smiled. "Oh, hello, beautiful. I'm glad you're awake. Let's check to see if we have your drugs right, shall we?" Miller held up a handheld camera and turned off the video that was running. Liam tried to understand. Miller had filmed himself torturing James?

Miller traveled soft hands down Liam's body. Liam's

mind recoiled in disgust. Miller's touch slowed at his hip and he used his fingertips to trace a line to Liam's cock. The man circled Liam's limp cock with one hand and pumped his shaft several times before he lowered his head and sucked Liam into his mouth.

Liam panted through the humiliation. He knew this torture well. Miller would start every session bringing Liam's cock to a state of arousal against his will. The act violated Liam like no other could and proved he had no control against Miller's vile actions. There was nothing he could do to stop his tormentor. His cock didn't remain flaccid. The drugs prevented muscle movement, but not the engorgement of blood to his cock because of the stimulus Miller provided.

"Still such a good boy for me, Liam." Miller stood over his chest. "I missed you, my beautiful lover—so much." Miller lowered and pressed his lips against Liam's. "I know. I know. It's been so long. I need to be in you, and I know you want me. You always respond so strongly to me, don't you?" Miller grasped Liam's cock and stroked him.

Miller lifted and smiled. "Did you hear? I found your bastard of a boss. I wanted you to see what I did to avenge you. I recorded it. Here, let me play it while I get you ready. We want you perfect when we make love. Don't we, darling?"

Miller placed the camera on a tray table and adjusted it so it was directly in Liam's line of sight. He pushed Play and walked away.

The tinny recording sounded out. Liam couldn't close his eyes, but he tried to avert them from his boss's naked body. "I could just sever your jugular. Simple and quick. Wash my hands of you." Miller turned the camera, cocked an eyebrow and sneered before he focused back on Caleb. "But that would be too good for a piece of shit like you. After all, you were actually responsible for taking Liam away from me to begin with, weren't you? No, I'm going to enjoy this. Let me tell you what I'm going to do." Miller tapped the scalpel on Caleb's shoulder as he paused. "No, no… no. That wouldn't be enough." Miller grabbed the camera and made sure his face was on the video before he spoke. "Oh, Liam, love, you need to watch this. Knowing you can't stop anything I'm going to do to the man who took you from me has to be—oh, I don't know—hard?"

A maniacal laugh filled the room. Both the recorded Miller and the flesh-and-blood Miller laughed. Liam's peripheral vision picked up Miller stringing tubing to an enema bag. The recording droned on as the camera zoomed in to a close-up and followed the scalpel. Caleb's chest lifted and fell in rapid succession as Miller used the knife to make an incision from his victim's breastbone to his navel, leaving a crimson path of blood. The bastard pulled the incision open before he leaned over Caleb. "Oh, poor man. Did that hurt? I hope it did. You have to be punished for taking the one destined to be mine forever away from me. He's mine. Forever. Shame on you for trying to take away what God gave me."

Miller stopped speaking for a few seconds before he almost shouted, "Hey, I know! Instead of just lopping these off, I'll open your nut sack, push out one teste at a time, and dissect them. That might not kill you, but if I cut deep around your cock, severing the veins that feed it? Oh! Or maybe I'll nick the femoral artery. That could do it! Sounds like a plan. That's what we'll do, okay?" The flat blade of the scalpel bounced off Caleb's lower stomach as Miller looked into the camera and smiled. "This is for taking my Liam, you bastard."

The horror-filled screams that followed brought bile to the back of Liam's throat. Liam panted fast, shallow breaths. His vision tunneled and a bliss-filled darkness started to encroach. The sound of the video floated away, distant and weak.

Miller's voice right beside him pulled at him. "Now, darling, we can't have you drifting off. A little something to keep you with me. After all, I need to see the love in your eyes." Liam saw a syringe pulled from the IV port. "Did you hear what I did to him?"

Liam's heartbeat sped up and he felt like he couldn't breathe. The drugs Miller gave him simultaneously froze and sped him up.

Miller talked to him, but he couldn't concentrate on the words. The feel of the man's hands against his feet startled Liam. A sharp pain zapped through the sole of his right leg and Liam tried desperately not to move. The drugs were wearing off and a weird electrical current of sensation pricked all his nerve endings. Miller had to have seen his muscles jump.

"No, that won't do. Your weight gain is affecting the mix. You need more."

A single solid noise, almost resembling the slamming of a cabinet door, sounded from somewhere to Liam's right. The muted sound drew his tormentor's attention. Miller's murmured comments turned into a hissed draw of air. The man darted from Liam's view. Carefully, Liam moved his head, jerky and spasmodic, but movement nonetheless.

Liam trained his eyes on Miller, who stood listening at the door. Carefully watching to make sure Miller wouldn't notice, he inched his right arm toward the IV pole that fed his body. The back of Liam's hand hit the cold metal. With everything he had, Liam pushed. The stand rocked and fell, pulling the IV needle free from his arm.

Miller's voice floated in from his right. The man moved away from the door toward him. Miller's whispered threat drifted toward Liam.

"For that, you die, my love."

Liam's head jerked an inch or so to the right, his focus on the door. Someone was out there. Liam prayed it wasn't Steele. Miller wouldn't go down easy. He glanced at Miller and caught sight of the gun in his hand, pointing Liam's way. A sense of complete serenity flushed over him. He felt his lips move. The smile was one of relief. He was going to die. He prayed Steele would understand that Liam didn't blame him. Nothing would have stopped Miller. The direction of his life had been determined five years ago.

Liam focused on the door. A huge crash sent shards of glass through the air. Liam watched transfixed as the gun Miller held bucked. Liam felt the bullet hit his chest. White-hot pain tore trenches of agony through his body. He tried to breathe, but the excruciating jolts of pain... God, they hurt. Liam's vision slowly tunneled. The blinding light of the room was blocked, no longer a torment. The pressure in his chest tightened, making his panting gasps futile. Liam stopped trying to breathe. The peace and warmth that enveloped him, held him and supported him seemed so right. Yes, it was time. He stopped fighting. In the midst of his pain, his last thoughts were of Steele—the man's warmth and kindness. Liam's love for Steele seemed almost tangible. Something he should be trying to seize. Liam attempted to cling to those thoughts—to the only good in his life—but along with the pain, the torment, and the fear, everything... ceased.

CHAPTER 20

*S*teele waited outside the door. He could hear movement and mumbled comments. They'd agreed on a quick diversion so Steele could enter the room and swing to his right. If it was Miller, he'd be in the corner of the room closest to the door. Steele's body tensed, ready to go. The crash of the fifty-gallon trash can through an exterior window triggered his entry. The door slammed to the wall at the same time as the sound of a gunshot roared through the small room.

The killer didn't react to Steele's entry. Instead, Miller's concentration focused on killing the man on the dining room table. Miller leveled his gun to fire again at the same time Steele lifted his weapon. Steele aimed his automatic at center mass and emptied the clip. He watched Miller's tall, thin body jerk convulsively and fall forward. His head bounced off the table where Liam's prostrate body lay.

Steele thumbed the magazine release and reloaded as he approached the killer. He toed the gun away from the lifeless body and kicked it across the room. Hardin dropped a knee into the bastard's back and cuffed the corpse. The fucker wasn't going to hurt anyone again. Once his teammate had secured the threat, Steele holstered his weapon at the same time as he bolted to Liam's side.

"Fuck! Hardin, get help in here *now!*" Steele placed his hands over the hole in Liam's chest and pushed down. Liam's body lay ashen and still. "No! Fuck no. Liam, don't you dare leave me, damn it!" Steele felt for a pulse. It was there, thready and weak. "That's it, baby. Stay with me. It's over. We got him. We never have to worry about that bastard again." Steele heard the sirens. "Hurry, damn it! Hardin, get them in here!" Steele moved his fingers, feeling for the pulse he'd had moments ago. Nothing. "Fuck! Don't you leave me, Liam!"

Several pairs of hands pulled him away from Liam. He fought the assault until Hardin's face blocked his view of Liam. "Stop it! Damn it, chief, let them work. They're helping him. Come on. Get a grip, man."

Steele pushed Hardin off him and glanced around the room. EMTs swarmed Liam. Two were on the ground with Miller. They both stood and took off their gloves immediately, gloving up again moving to the table where Liam lay.

The room flooded with people—cops, agents, and EMTs —but Steele had never felt so alone. The flurry of activity around Liam suddenly stopped and every person took a step back.

A deep voice rumbled, "Clear!" and Steele watched Liam's body arc off the wooden table.

For a long moment, nobody moved. Then a woman's voice said the most beautiful words he'd ever heard. "We've got him back." The technicians lifted Liam to a stretcher and he was moving. Steele followed, but a paramedic blocked him from getting into the ambulance.

"We don't have room. If I take you, I leave someone who can help me keep him alive." The big bastard who pushed

Steele back away from the bus didn't know how close he was to death.

"Chief, come on. I got the car." Hardin pulled on his arm. Steele bolted to the vehicle and hit the lights and siren. Hardin put the car in gear and they were on the ambulance's ass in seconds.

"I told responding patrols where we'd be—for statements." Steele didn't give a flying fuck about the crime scene, the shooting or anything else, but he nodded. His agent had been solid during the situation.

"Miller had him not three hundred feet from us. The bastard was going to keep him there, under our noses." Steele screamed the rage-filled words at the windshield.

"Yeah, and he would have succeeded if you hadn't got pissed and pushed me into that door. I think someone is watching over your man, chief. So much had to go right to get him out of there alive and you did it. You got him out." Hardin braked radically and passed the ambulance as soon as the road widened. He ran blocker for the bus, clearing traffic and expediting their travel to the trauma center. How he knew which hospital they were taking Liam to Steele didn't even question.

"*We* did it. If you hadn't caused a diversion, he would have killed Liam and probably me." Steele shivered at the possibilities. Liam was still alive. The rig was still lit up like a roman candle. If Liam wasn't alive, they'd have run silent.

The undercover vehicle skidded to a stop in front of the emergency room doors and both men were out of the car, opening the back door of the bus before the damn thing came to a complete stop. The EMT team lowered the gurney to the asphalt. A woman straddled Liam, giving chest compressions. The electronic doors opened and yellow-garbed hospital personnel swarmed Liam. They rolled him into a side room and the doors shut. Steele pushed the door open, but a small nurse grabbed his arm. Surprisingly strong for her stature, the nurse wedged herself between Steele and the door.

"Sir, you can't go back there. You'd be in the way. Let them work. I promise as soon as anyone knows anything, we'll let you know. Look. You can sit over here behind the nurse's station. It's out of the general population and when the other officers arrive, there will be room for all of you."

Steele finally looked down at the little woman. Her frizzy blonde hair stuck up in rampant curls, framing her heart-shaped face. "Other officers?" His mind wasn't online. Liam was behind those doors and that was the only thing he could concentrate on.

"Sir, you're covered in blood. You have a shoulder holster, badge and a gun, you came in a car with blue flashing lights, so I'm taking you for one of the good guys. I know you came straight from whatever shit got that man in there hurt. I've been a nurse in the ER long enough to know the follow-on of cops coming for statements and standing vigil will be sizable. So how about we get you set up over here? I can bring you some clean clothes—well, actually hospital scrubs—but that's better than being covered in blood, right?"

Steele's head went north and south as the feisty little pixie led him to a row of chairs. She pulled the seats out away from the wall and turned to look toward the door. Not satisfied, she grabbed ahold of the side of the chair and tugged, moving the entire bench about three feet. The metal base of the row of seats made a horrible screeching noise.

The little woman turned and surveyed the view. "There. Now you can sit down and watch the door." Steele's mind raced with the events of the night. A finger snapped in front of his face brought his attention to her small hand. "Hey! Yeah, you. Sit your ass down before you fall down. You're too damn big for me to catch. Now sit!" The feisty little munchkin pointed to the chair. Steele's ass planted in the hard plastic. "Good. I'm going to get you a change of clothes and find a place where you can grab a quick shower." Steele started to object, but she held up a hand. "I'm not going to make you leave until you know more about your friend."

"Partner." Steele's voiced cracked.

"Oh. I'm sorry. Your work is dangerous and you guys take risks every day. Thank you."

The sincerity in her voice cracked the hold he had on his sanity. Steele shook his head. "No, he's my boyfriend... my partner. My work partner is upstairs in the ICU. That bastard tried to kill both of them."

The tiny woman lowered in front of him until he looked at her. "Mister, those colleagues of mine are the best at what they do. Don't you give up on him, because I can guarantee they won't. I'll be back with news as soon as there is any." She lifted off the floor and patted his shoulder.

Steele felt the tears and he was damned if he could stop them. Instead, he dropped his head to his hands and prayed. Hardin made an appearance in his field of vision, but Steele didn't look up. His teammate sat down beside him and the man dropped an arm on his back. No words, just contact, and it was perfect. Steele needed something to ground him.

～

Steele's ass had permanently formed to the hard plastic. He'd given his statement and answered the questions—over and over and over. His supervisor and the FBI public relations team had showed up and left. They'd taken Liam to surgery and Steele had transferred from one piece of hard fucking plastic chair to another—different floor tile but the same fear as the minutes dragged by.

The pixie piranha, as he'd taken to calling the little nurse who fluttered in and out of the waiting rooms, had forced him into a vacant room and demanded he shower. She threatened a hazmat team response if he balked. He was in and out in record time. He glued his ass to the hard plastic again and watched the door. Coffee appeared, cooled and disappeared. People spoke. He wasn't sure if he answered.

The fucker had shot Liam. Hardin or Fleming said the gun Miller used was a .22 caliber. If it had been a nine mil or, God forbid, a .45, Liam wouldn't have lived this long. But even the force of the small-caliber bullet was enough to scramble the shit out of his chest cavity. *Fuck, stop it. You don't know how badly he's hurt.*

Steele jumped when the door opened. He always did, but this time a doctor came through the door and Steele rose.

"I'm looking for the family of Liam Mercier?" the doctor's tired voice called.

"I'm his boyfriend, Steele McKenzie." Steele braced himself for the physician's words.

"Oh. Next of kin?" The doctor looked from Steele to Hardin to Fleming. As if coordinated, all three palmed their badges and flashed them.

"Oh. Okay, right then. Well, it was touch and go for a while. The bullet split in two and nicked the left lung and lodged in the heart. We were able to repair the damage to the lung and the laceration to the heart muscle. The second piece of the bullet lodged against the spinal column. We removed it and we don't think there will be any permanent damage. We had to open his chest to make sure we repaired all the damage from the lacerations the bullet caused. Right now he's alive, but the prognosis isn't good."

Steele's knees buckled at the doctor's words. Hardin caught his elbow and kept him vertical.

"Can I see him?" The gravel in Steele's voice made it sound foreign, even to his ears.

The doctor pulled his surgical cap off. "Yeah, as soon as we get him transferred I'll send an orderly down for you. If he has any family, you probably need to get them here."

Steele nodded and watched the doctor walk back through the doors. "Angela, he has a brother—a homicide detective in Atlanta. Find him. Get word to him. Ask him to call Liam's parents."

"On it, chief." She grabbed her coat and headed out the door.

"He's alive, chief. He wouldn't be if you hadn't kept pushing." Hardin's words held little comfort.

"You heard the doc. He doesn't think..." Steele couldn't say the words. That would make Liam's mortality too real.

"I know. We do know what Miller had already done to him, what he'd be doing now if we hadn't stopped him. Do you honestly think Liam would have wanted that over this? At least now he can fight. He didn't have that option against Miller." Hardin nodded toward the door. "I'm going to check on Masterson and give you a minute to pull your shit together before they take you in to see Liam. I'll be back."

Steele nodded and slid back into that piece of shit plastic hospital chair. The cold fear that had gripped him while Liam had been in surgery wrapped around his soul and settled against his heart. Death was trying to seize his beautiful man. His angel. Steele clasped his hands and bowed his head. The words weren't pretty. He didn't know how to do it right, but with everything he had, he petitioned God on Liam's behalf.

"I have always believed in You. I *know* You exist. I know You can't hate what You create. That man is Your creation. He has literally been through hell on earth. Please, show Your compassion and grant him life." Steele's tears anointed his desperate prayer.

CHAPTER 21

he waiting area for the ICU was a different version of the same hell. Steele waited for the charge nurse to come get him. The orderly said she would when they had Liam settled. When the stainless steel doors opened, the nurse finally led him back to where he scrubbed up with some foul-smelling disinfectant soap. Steele used the brush provided and washed thoroughly, determined not to bring anything that could hurt Liam into the ICU. He slipped on protective clothing and followed the nurse into the unit. Five beds circled a central nurse's station.

The nurse led him to Liam. He paused in the entryway and swallowed back the emotion that welled up when he saw his angel. Tubes and wires crisscrossed the air between his lover and the machines that monitored him. There wasn't a machine breathing for him. Steele thanked God for that.

The nurse pulled up a small, wheeled stool. "Here. You can sit here. I'll work around you during my shift. The swing shift nurse is my friend. She'll let you stay. Midnight shift? That woman is brutal, but if I can get the doc to say it's cool for you to be here, she can stick it."

Steele smiled for the first time in what felt like years. "Thank you." He moved his focus forward on Liam—his beautiful Liam. He swung a glance at the nurse and asked, "May I touch him?"

She smiled and nodded. "Anywhere he's not hooked to a machine. Talk to him. We've got him sedated so he can heal. The doc probably won't bring him further out of it until his vitals get stronger. Right now, he's fighting to stay with us. I'll be in every couple of minutes, but you pretend like I'm not here."

Steele took a tentative step toward Liam. The man looked so damn fragile. Steele sat on the low stool and carefully picked up Liam's hand. It was cold to the touch. Steele cupped it in both of his. Liam hated being cold. He'd get more blankets the next time the nurse stopped in.

Steele whispered, "Hey, angel. You made it out of surgery. I need you to keep trying, baby. You need to come back to me. I don't want to be here without you." Steele snuffed back his tears. "Hell, I know it's probably premature, and I'm freaking myself out by saying it, but I think I'm in love with you, Liam." Steele moved the stool closer and dropped his head onto the bed beside Liam's arm. "No, that's not true. I *know* I'm in love with you." A small sob hitched in his chest. Steele lifted his face to wipe the tears away. He looked up at Liam's face. "Pathetic, huh? I mean, you just came into my life, but I can't imagine a future without you in it." Steele laid his head on the side of the bed, his cheek against Liam's hand. "Come back to me, baby. Please."

$\approx$

THE HOURS—THEN days—ran into each other. Nurses changed, doctors came in and out and Steele learned to become a wallflower so he wasn't asked to leave. Karen, the day nurse, had forced him to get a shower and eat something. She'd put his cell phone number in hers so she could call if anything happened while he was gone. It was the only reason he agreed to leave, even for a few minutes.

Sometime during the swirl of time, a chair with a back had been placed next to Liam's bed. Steele said a silent prayer of thanks to whomever the nurses had to bribe to get the chair into the ICU.

Steele checked on Masterson. His partner had been moved out of the ICU when Liam was in surgery. Lucifer had Sam placed in a private suite and had brought in reconstructive specialists for the agent's severely damaged hands and face.

Steele waited for Karen to finish her checks on Liam before he sat down. Liam's color had improved—a little. The doctors guarded their comments. Liam had lived through that first critical twenty-four hours after his surgery. According to the bitchy midnight shift nurse, they really hadn't thought he would. Steele took Liam's hand in his and kissed the back of it. His angel was strong.

"I saw you on television when Liam gave the statement at the press conference."

Steele's head whipped to the side at the comment. His eyes bounced from the man in the door to the man on the bed. They could have been twins, except the man in the door had brown hair and was taller than Liam.

"Aiden?" Steele's question croaked out. He cleared his throat and tried again. "Are you Aiden?"

The man nodded. "I am. Is he going to live?"

Steele turned back to his lover and pushed Liam's hair away from his face tenderly. "He's fighting."

"Who are you?" Liam's brother walked into the room but didn't touch his brother. His eyes roamed over Liam.

"Special Agent Steele McKenzie. His partner." Steele met

the man's eyes, defying him to say something—anything homophobic.

"FBI? How long has he worked with you?" Aiden crossed his arms over his chest and waited for a reply.

"Not that kind of partner. We're in a relationship. Do you have a problem with that?" The challenge dropped from his lips and he braced for the answer.

"Oh. Liam's gay? I mean, obviously, but..." Aiden's face flushed red. His coloring was light like Liam's, despite the darker hair.

"But?" Steele prompted.

Aiden pulled his hand through his short brown hair. "Our parents told me Liam left. Told me he was lost to sin and he didn't want to see any of us again. Said he was dead to them. I didn't know."

Steele dropped into the chair and shook his head. Exhaustion overwhelmed him. "They told him to leave because he was gay. He said he tried to contact you, but he didn't get a response."

Aiden took a tentative step forward and brushed his fingertips against Liam's arm. "He tried?"

Steele nodded. "He did."

"After I escaped that hell, I tried to find him. I couldn't dig up anything on him. It was like he'd dropped off the face of the earth. Then I was watching television one night and there he was. I pulled the interview up on the computer and saved it so I'd have a link to him. I called the local FBI office. I've worked with several of the agents in Atlanta. I asked them for help, but they ran into a stone wall. No one knew where he was."

"Protective custody until we caught Stuart Miller." Steele's thumb caressed the back of Liam's hand in small circles.

"The news said Miller was killed."

"Yes."

"You kill him?"

Steele lifted his eyes and leveled a gaze at Liam's brother. "I emptied nine .45 slugs into that bastard and I would have reloaded and emptied it again if Liam hadn't been hurt."

Aiden grunted. "Good."

"Did you call your parents?" Steele cringed at the thought. The cold-hearted assholes could show up, claim a familial tie, and throw Steele out on his ear. Hell, so could Aiden.

"Nope. Don't intend on talking to them in this lifetime. The agent who contacted me said it was urgent. I took a leave of absence from APD and drove up here. Didn't know how this—between Liam and I would go down. Never thought it would be like this." Aiden cleared his throat and put his hands in his pockets.

"Look, I just got into town. I'm going to get a room at a hotel, then I'll be back. Maybe relieve you for a couple hours so you can do whatever you need to do."

"Give me a couple minutes and I'll get an agent here. He'll take you to my apartment. There's a guest room. If you're going to stay, you might as well stay with us." Steele reached in his pocket and handed Aiden his apartment keys.

"Oh, and feed the cat, would you? My team is taking turns checking on him."

Aiden's eyebrows shot up. "Cat?"

"Yeah, his name's Phil."

CHAPTER 22

*L*iam knew that voice. The deep rumble held him and soothed the fear. He was so tired. He knew he could stop fighting, but Steele's words kept him from floating back into the darkness that hovered not too far away. Liam didn't want to let go. He knew it would be easier, but he needed to let Steele know he was okay. A shot of pain laced up his chest. Fuck, *that* hurt. Liam tried to open his eyes, but for some reason the concept was beyond him. He felt a soothing repetitive caress on his hand. The soft contact was nice. He concentrated on the motion and slipped back into oblivion.

~

CONSCIOUSNESS CAME IMMEDIATELY, and fuck did it hurt. Liam's muscles seized tight against the pain. A groan escaped.

"Hey, Liam. Steele's going to be pissed he wasn't here."

Liam blinked, trying to bring the person in front of him

into focus. A shot of fire ran through his chest and he clenched his eyes, hissing in pain.

"Hang on, I'll get the nurse."

The man's voice was familiar, but he hurt too damn bad to try to figure out why.

"Ah, Mr. Mercier, the doctor said you could have some more pain medication when you came around. Are you hurting?" The female's happy sing-song voice grated against Liam like metal brushes against exposed nerves.

"Yes." The word ground out through his locked jaw.

"Alright. Let's get you comfortable again then, shall we?"

Liam heard the woman moving but kept his eyes closed. Hospital. He was in a hospital. His mind raced. Miller! Fuck! He had to get to Steele!

"Steele?" He opened his eyes and blinked wildly, trying to bring the room into focus.

"Liam, relax. He's okay. He'll be here soon."

"He's okay?" A wave of complete contentment hit Liam and his body relaxed. God, that was awesome. He was flying. Liam blinked and focused on the person standing beside him.

"Yeah, he's fine."

Aiden. Aiden was beside the hospital bed. Liam smiled. He rolled his head and found the nurse. "Hey, did you know I'm hallucinating? I'm seeing my brother."

The nurse laughed and he felt her hand pat his shoulder. "You enjoy that ride, Mr. Mercier. We'll get you comfortable and level out your meds. Right now, though, I think you'll probably need to sleep."

Liam rolled his head back to where he thought he'd seen his brother and smiled as the world slipped away. "Okay."

~

LIAM WOKE to the sounds of the hospital—the steady beeping of a heart monitor, the shuffle of soft-soled shoes against tile flooring, a hushed murmur of voices and the clack of metal against metal. He'd recognize the symphony of sounds anywhere. A soft, gentle touch stroked rhythmically up and down his arm. Liam turned his head and opened his eyes. Steele's head lay beside his fingers. His hand traveled up and down Liam's arm. Liam lifted his fingers to card them through Steele's dark hair.

Steele bolted upright and grabbed Liam's hand.

"Oh thank God! I thought I'd lost you. Liam, I love you."

Liam tried to speak, but Steele shushed him. "I know it's quick. You don't have to say it back, but you've got to know how I feel. I love you." Steele's lips pressed against Liam's. The warmth of the chaste kiss settled over Liam and wrapped him in a feeling he thought he'd lost forever.

"I love you too. Miller?" Liam whispered against his lover's lips.

"He's gone. Dead. He'll never hurt you or anyone else ever again." Steele's forehead lay against his. The simple act brought tears to Liam's eyes.

"You sure?" Steele would understand. He'd know why Liam asked, had to know.

"Positive. I watched his corpse go into the crematorium. He's dead. Gone. I made sure of it, for both of us. He can't hurt us again."

Liam's tears fell hot against his cheeks. He didn't try to hide them—not from Steele.

"Are you hurting?" Steele pushed Liam's hair out of his face.

"No. Water?" Liam's words were barely above a whisper.

"Ice chips until the doc says I can give you more." Steele lifted a spoon full of ice to his lips. Liam let the chips melt on his tongue, savoring the cool moisture.

"Better than Scotch."

"Well, enjoy it; I don't think you'll be getting any Scotch anytime soon."

Liam leaned back, but then his eyes popped open and he grabbed at Steele's arm. "Sam? Is Sam alive?"

Steele brushed Liam's hair away from his face with a tender touch. "Yeah, angel, he's going to be okay. He's had two surgeries already. Lucifer has the best surgeons here for him."

"Lucifer?"

"Yeah, evidently they are a thing. The man put Sam in a private suite so he can stay with him. Sam has the best care money can buy. He's paying for this room too."

"Why?"

"Sam was worried about you. Lucifer told him he'd take care of everything and that man is impossible to stop once he gets into daddy mode."

Liam chuckled, his eyes drifting shut. "Daddy mode? Sam's got some kink to explain."

Steele's warm lips drifted over his forehead. "Yeah, but we'll give him some space. You rest now."

Liam tried to push away the exhaustion that was claiming him. "Steele?"

"I'm here, baby. Not leaving." Steele's hand resumed its slow caress of his arm. The tranquil, relaxed feeling added to his sensation of floating.

"My brother. Was he here?"

From a long distance, he somehow understood Steele telling him, "Yeah, angel, he's here."

CHAPTER 23

"What? Yeah... No, wait just a minute. Okay, I got them all up. The latest victim was found where?"

Liam blinked at Steele's voice. The pain in his chest was still there but distant—no longer overwhelming him. Liam rolled his head and tried to understand what he was seeing. A wall. Obviously. Damn, what was up with the crime scene photos taped on the wall in his hospital room? Liam looked down at the thick, furry blanket that covered his legs. It had patterns of small kittens playing with yarn printed all over it. That was new. Steele taking care of him again. There were fresh flowers on the metal stand next to him. Purple balloons tied to a huge stuffed teddy bear sat on the chair in the corner of the room. Steele had told him the bear was a substitute because he couldn't bring Phil to visit. God, he fucking loved his man.

Steele's voice pulled Liam's attention back to the far side of the room. "No, no I got it. Get on the last interview and email it to me when you get it typed up. Huh? No, not yet.

Yeah. Get Fleming to harass the forensics team for that DNA analysis. Right. Be in contact."

Steele slid his phone into his pocket. Liam tried to speak, but Steele's mutterings silenced him before he got the words to form. Steele stood with his back to Liam and talked to the wall.

"Okay, you four, what in the hell do you have in common? Why would he choose you? You don't work together. You don't all go to any school in common. You're not the same sex, the same race or the same sexual orientation. No similar spending habits. Not the same socioeconomic class. Two went to the same clubs to a party but two didn't. One was deeply religious. No emails or text messages that link you to each other or to anyone in your past, yet all four of you were found bound, gagged, strangled and dumped in the same campground miles from where any of you lived. None of you owned cars. How did you get out there? Why didn't anyone see you? Nothing ties any of you to the campground where you were found. The woman who owns it is sixty-five years old, less than a hundred pounds, single and lives with a buttload of cats. No way she's the killer. What in the hell am I missing here?"

Liam looked at the pictures on the wall. The young faces on the wall were of similar age. Social media. That's where he'd look for a lead. Liam closed his eyes and swallowed, or actually, he tried to swallow. His throat felt like he'd crossed the desert, during a drought, while eating sawdust. He peeled his tongue off the roof of his mouth and winced at the horrid taste. Morning breath had nothing on medicine breath. Liam scanned the room. There. Water. It was so cold that there was sweat on the outside of the cup. Oh sweet fuck, the only thing he wanted more than Steele was a drink of that water. He reached out, trying not to lift too far off the bed. Amazing how weak he still felt. Shit, the stand was just out of his grasp.

Liam winced. He'd stretched too far, and holy hell, he wasn't going to do that again. Liam looked down at his chest and pulled his hospital gown away. The railroad track going down the center of his chest was the cause of his discomfort. Thankfully, the reach hadn't pulled any stitches or started anything bleeding. Steele would be on his ass in a second for that. Hell, he'd been there and gotten the T-shirt. The doc said the stitches wouldn't leave much of a scar, but the lateral…well, shit. The realization that the incision was going to leave a foot-long scar down the middle of his chest hit him as funny. Liam couldn't help it. He started laughing. Like *he* needed to worry about one more scar, no matter how big.

"Hey, angel, you're finally awake." Steele was suddenly by his side. The smile on Steele's face and the raw emotion he saw in the blue depths made up for his lack of attention.

"Hey." His mouth and tongue felt like they were wrapped in cotton batting.

"How are you feeling? Are you in pain? I can call the nurse." Steele reached for the call button.

"No, I'm okay. I need water." Liam nodded toward the cup.

Steele grabbed the plastic container and dropped a straw in the top. Liam drew at least half of the ice water through the straw before he stopped.

Liam rolled his eyes as he drank. Taking a breath, he praised the liquid. "That was almost orgasmic." It really wasn't an exaggeration. He'd had sex that hadn't given him that much pleasure—though not with Steele, of course. Sex with his man was phenomenal, but with some of the others he'd hooked up with? Meh… at best.

"Good to know." Steele's laughter bounced around the room. Liam smiled and drank the rest of the water.

"How did my room turn into your office?" Liam motioned toward the wall.

"Well, that's an interesting story. Hardin and Fleming are in Arizona, flew there on the red eye last night. The state police called us in when they found a body dump site. Four corpses so far. Same MO but no connection between the victims. The kills are recent. Two of the victims haven't been reported as missing yet. And the reason your wall is now my office is simple. If I work this at the office at the Bureau, I don't get to spend time with you. So ipso facto, I moved in."

"The nurses going to be okay with that?" Liam nodded toward the graphic crime scene photos.

"With what Lucifer is paying them? I think so." Steele sat on the side of Liam's bed and leaned down for kiss.

"Medicine breath."

"Don't care." Steele's warm lips swept over Liam's, his hands cupping Liam's face. Liam shuddered and leaned into the gentle sweep of Steele's lips.

"I can't wait to get you home, in my bed." Steele's hot breath carried the soft words to Liam.

"Maybe when you spring me from this place, I can handle things for you?" Liam moved his hands under Steele's suit jacket. His man's hard pecs felt so right. He found Steele's nipples tight and taut under his dress shirt. He tweaked the nubs and Steele's hips bucked forward. His head dropped to Liam's shoulder. Liam palmed Steele's heavy cock and created some friction for his man.

"Fuck, baby, you can handle me anytime you want when we get home." Steele's weight on his shoulder felt so damn good. He was being released sometime this afternoon and Liam was past ready. He needed a shower, not the bullshit handheld spigot and the metal chair with a drain in the floor. No, Liam wanted a real shower with a blow job. That would be the goal. Not for him, for Steele. His libido had taken a little vacation. The doctors had said that sometimes happened after major surgeries, but that didn't mean Steele needed to suffer. Besides, his doctor had threatened to keep him at the hospital if he didn't behave. Behaving, by the doctor's standards, included no anal sex or anything that would rub or cause pressure to his chest cavity. Even with those restrictions, Liam was left with one hell of a lot of things he could do to keep his agent happy.

"Just a couple more hours." Liam kept an eye on the closed door and undid Steele's slacks. The hiss of air that escaped from his man put a smirk on his face.

"You like that?" Liam pulled Steele's cock out and gripped the length, sliding his hand up to the mushroom head. He thumbed Steele's slit and pushed down his shaft again.

"Fuck!" Steele shifted to rest his weight on his arms. That gave Liam's arm the freedom to move and make his grasp of Steele's cock less awkward.

Liam stroked Steele's weeping shaft, catching the small sounds of desire his man was making. "Going to get you to masturbate for me, Steele. Want to see you laid out on our bed. Going to watch you use your hand to make yourself explode. I want to see your cum shoot up your stomach. Then I'm going to have you lift over me so I can lick it off your chest."

Steele groaned a curse and pressed forward for a kiss, his lips sweeping over Liam's. Steele's tongue asked for entrance, but Liam denied him, biting down on Steele's bottom lip instead. He pressed his thumbnail into Steele's slit. The zing of pressure was enough to send Steele over the edge. Liam loved the way Steele held his breath, his entire body clenched hard as he came in Liam's fist.

Liam waited until Steele's pulses stopped. He lifted his fist to his face, and while staring straight into Steele's eyes, he licked a tongue-full of Steele's cum into his mouth and swallowed.

"Jesus, you're a dirty, sexy man, Liam Mercier. Have I told you today how much I love you?"

"Not in words." Liam held up his hand and smiled before he leaned up for a kiss.

"I love you, Liam. You are everything to me. Nothing I do means anything if you're not in my world. When they told me you might not make it… I was going to walk away from the Bureau. I couldn't face a daily reminder of my failure to protect the man I love." Steele reached over and grabbed some tissue to clean himself.

"I love you too. What do you mean, your failure to protect me?" Liam watched Steele tuck himself back in his slacks and go into the bathroom, returning with a damp washcloth to wipe off the rest of his cum from Liam's hand. Steele concentrated on cleaning Liam's fingers, acting as if the act of washing was the most important thing in the world.

Finally Steele shrugged. "I left you alone. Miller walked in and took you from me."

"Miller was in the compound before he called you. He was probably in the house when you were making plans to get Sam. If you'd taken me with you, he would have waited until we got back. You'd be dead and I'd have been in his hands, which is worse than dead. Face it. Someone was watching out for both of us."

"I get that. Rationally, what you're telling me I understand. But my gut is telling me I failed you—something I need to work on."

"We both have baggage, issues we need to deal with."

"We do, and we will. Together." Steele lowered and kissed Liam. The sweep of Steele's tongue over his lips caused a shiver and his dick stirred a little. Good signs.

"Oh, good." Steele raised that eyebrow again. Fuck, that was so sexy.

"My body liked that kiss." Liam could feel the fire burning under his skin. Damn blushes.

"Just liked it?" Steele's dark eyebrows danced and Liam's breath caught in his chest.

"Loved it."

"Oh, that's real good." Steele kissed him again, this time dropping his hand to Liam's cock.

It definitely noticed the attention.

"I'm going to be good now and walk away."

"First for you?"

"Damn straight. Has to be because I'm in love. Been doing all sorts of strange shit."

"Oh yeah? Like what?"

"Taking care of a stealth-mode, ninja-wannabe attack cat."

"Point."

"Two. I get double for that."

"Agreed. Two points."

Steele laughed and turned to rinse off the washcloth when the door to the room opened.

"God, you'd think I could get away from murder boards." Aiden's voice from the doorway pulled their gazes from each other. A couple minutes earlier and his brother might have caught Steele in an embarrassing situation.

Liam had spoken to his brother a couple of times, but equating the gangly teenager he remembered and the man he was eleven years later threw him. But in the week since he'd thought he'd hallucinated seeing Aiden, they'd covered some serious emotional ground. Their parents had fucked them both over. Liam couldn't deal with pulling the physical and emotional abuse they'd suffered out into the light of day, but he knew they'd talk about it... eventually.

"Kinda comes with the territory when you're rooming with the team leader for the FBI's Serial Killer Task Force." Liam was proud of his man.

"Yeah, well, let's just say I wasn't expecting crime scene photos on your hospital wall. You okay with that? I mean, after what you've been through?" Aiden stared straight at Steele, his tone more accusatory than inquisitive.

Liam swallowed hard. For so long he'd been alone—well, except for Phil—and now he had two men growling protectively over him. "The only crime scene photos I've ever had an issue with were Miller's. This? I can deal with this. Besides, I was just about to help Steele with this one."

Steele wasn't mollified. "Let's get something straight right here and now, Aiden. I would never do anything to hurt this man. He knows what I do. We've talked about our future together and what that entails. Neither you nor anyone else has the right to question my love for, or loyalty to, this man... ever. Are we clear?" His face turned a dark shade of crimson and his voice shook with anger as he ground out his warning.

"Crystal clear, Agent McKenzie. My concern is for my brother's mental health, not the status of your relationship, but thank you very much for pissing all over him. I get it. He's yours." Aiden moved the bear and balloons to a small dresser and sat in the chair. Liam had to admit his brother was kind of a badass. Aiden threw a definite vibe and the 'don't fuck with me' attitude shone through with neon fluorescent clarity.

"Damn straight he is." Steele's glare hadn't waivered.

"Not my business." Aiden shrugged his shoulders.

"And it never was."

"Noted."

"Fine."

Liam pushed himself up in the bed, making the move

without wincing... much. Both Steele and Aiden started toward the bed, but Liam lifted his hand, stilling both of them. "I got it. Thanks."

"Back to the wall." That comment got Aiden a glare from Steele.

"What about it?" Liam watched Steele tense.

"What's the story? Obviously, it's a serial killer or you wouldn't be assigned. What's the story?"

Steele turned toward the photos and ran Aiden through the facts they knew.

"So there is no connection." Aiden shuffled through the paperwork Steele had lying on a stainless steel tray table.

"None that we could find."

Liam cleared his throat. His insecurities about helping Steele were front and center. Hopefully, with continued therapy, Liam would be surer of himself, but he'd take it one day at a time. Finally, he spoke. "Steele, have you looked at social media? Find out what platforms all four of them were on. See if there are any similarities."

Steele rubbed the back of his neck, a mannerism Liam recognized that he fell back on when he was tense and thinking. "I already ran the big three, babe. Nothing on Facebook, Twitter or Instagram. Nothing."

Liam shook his head. "Then look for the abstract. Snapchat, Grindr, Tinder, Tumblr, Uber. Check their phones, tablets and computers. They might not have all apps on all three. Hell, didn't one of the dating sites have three significant security breaches in one year? Maybe someone was able to use a breach in coding of one of the apps they all used to locate the victims."

Aiden and Steele both turned and looked at Liam as if he had three heads.

"What? It was just a thought."

Steele pulled his phone out of his pocket as he made the

trip across the room. "A fucking savant. That's what you are. I love you, baby. I'm going to go outside where the reception is better. Taxis or common rides could be how he got to them and got them without anyone seeing anything." Steele kissed Liam hard and nearly ran out of the room.

Aiden walked over and sat at the end of Liam's bed. "You thinking about going back to the FBI when you're cleared?"

Liam pushed his hair back behind his ears and shook his head. "No. I'm okay with what Steele does, but I don't want to live this every day." Liam waved at the crime scene photos on the far wall. "We talked, and with Steele's pay and my disability, we'll be able to buy a house somewhere near his office. He'll eventually have to travel with his team again, so I need to work on integrating myself back into society. The thought of that terrifies me." Liam gave a sharp look at his brother and pointed his finger at his chest. "Don't you dare tell him I said that. He doesn't need to worry about me. Now that I know there is no way Miller..." Liam turned away from Aiden as the memories of that bastard slammed into his mind.

Aiden moved up the bed and grabbed Liam's hand. "Hey. It's all right. You've been through some serious shit."

Liam huffed at the understatement. "Beyond. Serious. Shit."

Aiden patted Liam's leg and cleared his throat. "So I was thinking maybe I'd move up here."

That caught Liam's attention. "Why? I mean, why would you leave your life in Atlanta?"

"Well, you said it yourself. Steele will eventually go on the road again. I could be up here in case you needed me. There's that, and I want to get to know you better. Nothing is tying me to Georgia, and from what I've seen, Virginia isn't that bad."

"I wouldn't know. Steele uprooted me from my self-imposed prison in Florida. But if Steele's here, I'm staying. It would be great to get to know you better, Aiden."

His brother's eyes were conspicuously moist as he stood and walked over to the window. Something drew his attention and he craned his neck for a moment. Chuckling, he turned back to Liam with a smile. "Your man's out there pacing back and forth, talking on the phone swinging his arms like a madman. Hopefully no one turns him in as an escapee from the asylum."

Liam's smile froze and he changed the subject. Aiden's comment triggered shards of ice-cold fear to stab through his gut. *Miller is dead.* Liam repeated the chant over and over in his head. Someday he might believe it, but today wasn't that day.

EPILOGUE

Steele unlocked the front door of his house and dropped the keys into the ceramic bowl on the table just inside the hall. He keyed his access code for the alarm and smiled as the aroma of something meaty and delicious hit him. Lemon herb-roasted chicken. Jesus, Liam knew how to spoil him. He'd been gone for over two weeks this time. The case was still active, but they were out of leads. Not every case had a happy ending. Hell, if half of them ended with the bad guy in cuffs or dead that would have been a win for Steele, but as Liam reminded him every night when they spoke, real agents faced real crimes, not the kind that could be solved in thirty minutes. And surprisingly, hearing that reassurance helped when he was beating his head against a brick wall. Sometimes the villain won.

He toed off his shoes and stripped out of his jacket, hooking it on the coat tree. The temperature of the house was a couple of degrees south of sweltering. It was something Steele could adapt to, but in order to do so, he usually stripped the minute he walked in the door from work. His tie and button-down were off next as he padded through the house in search of his man. Steele heard Liam's smoky voice and headed for the study after he dropped his clothes inside the laundry hamper in their room. Dressed in just his slacks and T-shirt, Steele grabbed up Phil, who'd left the study and was heading straight for him. The cat rumbled in his rough, motorboat fashion. A paw reached up and patted Steele's cheek. The affection still threw him for a loop, but the hellcat had mellowed with age—and if he was honest, so had he.

Liam sat behind his bank of computer monitors as he spoke to one of his students via video conference. He'd finished his doctoral degree and now taught classes online. If you believed the dean of students, Liam had single-handedly turned the university's stagnant criminal justice degree program into the most sought-after online course in the country. Steele couldn't be prouder of his man. Granted, even after two years, Liam didn't often leave the security of the house. But he'd made huge strides in his mental health. Liam lifted his gaze toward Steele and paused in his dialog before a slow, sexy smile spread across his face.

Steele smiled back and nodded out the door. Liam nodded and held up his hands indicating ten minutes. Steele gave his love a wink and headed toward the kitchen and hopefully an ice-cold beer. He dropped the ninja stealth cat on the kitchen floor and a handful of kitty kibble into the fat cat's bowl. Steele grabbed a beer and opened the door to the back porch, where he melted into a chaise lounge. The meticulously maintained backyard was also Liam's doing. Flowers and blooming plants of all shapes and sizes had been carefully planted and manicured until it looked like a magazine photo shoot. God, it was good to be home.

Steele chugged half of his IPA and closed his eyes. Happy didn't begin to describe his life. Getting to this point hadn't been easy. Liam's second abduction had left lasting mental scars that required a two-month inpatient stay so he and Dr.

Morgan could work through Liam's most debilitating issues. But they'd held together during that difficult time and had drawn strength from each other. In every conceivable way, they completed each other.

His cell vibrated and Steele smiled at the name on the face. "Sam, how the hell's it hanging?"

"Limp, but still bigger than yours." Sam's snide comment earned a chuckle from Steele.

"I'm not getting any complaints, asshole." Steele missed his work partner. Because of his physical injuries, the Bureau hadn't cleared Sam for return. So he'd worked freelance jobs for a local security firm before opening his own agency. Sam specialized in missing persons cases and had a couple of teams that worked throughout the nation.

"Liam's just settling."

"Bite me."

"Nah, your fiancé would get jealous." Sam chuckled.

"You're still coming, right?" Steele knew if he didn't keep on Sam, the man would find an excuse to miss his wedding. Sam hated the reactions of the people he used to work with. He looked nothing like the man who had gone on that ill-fated call. His face wasn't his own. The plastic surgeons were phenomenal with the reconstruction, but with the exception of his eyes, there was no way Steele would recognize Sam if he hadn't witnessed the dozens of surgeries for himself.

"Do I want to go? Hell no. But I won't be that guy. I'll stand with you when you finally make an honest man out him. Dr. and Mr. Mercier, right?"

"Fuck you, man. Mr. and Dr. McKenzie. His suggestion, not mine." Steele sent a silent thank you to the man above. Sam's professional success wasn't echoed in his personal life. He'd stopped all contact with Lucifer. Sam had succinctly told Steele to keep his fucking nose out of his personal business when he'd asked what had happened. Nobody ever called him stupid. Steele hadn't asked again.

"He's too good for you. But, there is no accounting for taste." The humor-filled jab got a laugh from Steele. He really missed his friend.

"I think I should take offense, but I won't. How're things?" Steele made sure he didn't step over the line, but he cared and Sam needed to know.

"Same shit, different day. Anyway, the reason I called was I'm holding a résumé in my hand that lists you as a reference."

Steele dropped the beer bottle he'd lifted to his lips. "Who?"

"Aiden Mercier."

"No shit?" Steele glanced up as Liam walked onto the porch. His man had a lightweight sweatshirt on but carried two bottles of beer. Liam lifted his eyebrows and gave a suggestive smile as he straddled Steele's hips. He leaned in for a quick kiss as Sam continued.

"Yeah, I thought he got a promotion to sergeant at the Atlanta P.D.?" Liam snuggled into Steele's chest, forcing him to think hard in order to remember what the hell he and Sam were talking about.

"He did. I don't know why he's applying up here, but I have no problem giving him my highest recommendation. The kid is sharp. My contacts at the Atlanta office all speak highly of him. I'll ask Liam if he knows what is going on, but dude, you wouldn't be wrong to hire him."

Liam lifted his head and gave Steele a questioning look. Steele mouthed 'Aiden' to him before he pulled his lover back against his chest. They both craved the contact. The personal intimacy they shared fed them both.

"Cool. If the kid is anything like his brother, he'll be an asset. I'm pulling the trigger on this."

"That works. I'll let Liam know. Hell, he may already know. I just got home from the field. Out two weeks in Utah."

"Resolution?"

"Nah. Left Fleming and Berry. They are working with the local office, but the leads are dead."

"How's Berry working out?"

"He's good, but he's never going to be you."

"Of course not. I'm irreplaceable."

"True that."

"I'm out. And before you ask again, I promise I'll be there."

"Cool. Take care, man."

"Always."

Steele ended the call as Liam caught his lips in a kiss. The warm sweep of Liam's tongue sent a shiver of desire through him. Liam laughed, the air following his tongue into Steele's mouth. He pulled back, but his fall of long blond hair formed a curtain around them.

"Hi, baby." Steele cupped Liam's neck and pulled him down for another kiss. Liam arched his back and rubbed his hardened length against Steele's groin. God, he needed his man.

"Hey." Liam lifted and smiled down at him. "What about Aiden?"

"He applied for a job with Sam's agency." Steele took a swig of the beer Liam had delivered to him.

"Did he? Huh." Liam lifted his beer and Steele took that opportunity to run his free hand under the layers of clothing, reaching the warmth of soft skin underneath.

"Mmm... do you know why?" Steele wasn't really interested in Aiden's story right now. His hand expertly unfastened Liam's jeans and dipped below his waistband, the hot tip of Liam's cock poking toward his fingers.

"Speculation only." Liam moved his hips forward, chasing the contact.

"Then speculate." Steele set the beer down on the decking of the porch and wrapped his hand around Liam's thigh.

"Either he wants to move closer to us, he likes the area, or there's someone up here he wants to be near."

"And which is it?" Steele's hand rose and applied pressure to Liam's balls. Not too much, just enough to make him want more.

"All three." Liam's answer came out as more of a groan than a reply.

"Is that so?"

"Mmm…" The man was lost to the sensations. Steele didn't care. Aiden was a big boy. A cop. He could deal. Steele slid his arm up Liam's back and wound a fist into his thick blond hair.

"Did you miss me?" Steele stopped Liam from kissing him by pulling back on his hair.

"God, you know I did. I need you." Liam panted just above Steele's mouth.

"I do know that. I know you need me, baby. Just relax. I'll take care of you."

"Promise me." Liam's whispered plea came millimeters above Steele's lips

"Forever. I promise you, my love, forever."

~The End~

ALSO BY KRIS MICHAELS

Jacob, The Kings of Guardian - Book One
Joseph, The Kings of Guardian - Book Two
Adam, The Kings of Guardian - Book Three
Jason, The Kings of Guardian - Book Four
Jared, The Kings of Guardian - Book Five
Jasmine, The Kings of Guardian - Book Six
Chief, The Kings of Guardian - Book Seven
Jewell, The Kings of Guardian - Book Eight
Jade, The Kings of Guardian - Book Nine

Guardian Security Shadow World Series:

Anubis

The Everlight Series:
An Evidence of Magic
An Incident of Magic

Stand Alone Novel:
A Heart's Desire

Made in the USA
Coppell, TX
01 September 2021